INTO THE
WEB

Also by Thomas H. Cook
in Large Print:

Peril
Places in the Dark
Instruments of Night

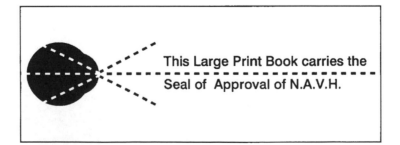

INTO THE WEB

THOMAS H. COOK

WHEELER
PUBLISHING

Published in 2004 by arrangement with Bantam Books, an imprint of the Bantam Dell Publishing Group, a division of Random House, Inc.

Wheeler Large Print Hardcover.

The text of this Large Print edition is unabridged.
Other aspects of the book may vary from the original edition.

Set in 16 pt. Plantin by Minnie B. Raven.

Printed in the United States on permanent paper.

Library of Congress Cataloging-in-Publication Data

Cook, Thomas H.
     Into the web / Thomas H. Cook.
       p. cm.
     ISBN 1-58724-820-4 (lg. print : hc : alk. paper)
     1. West Virginia — Fiction.   2. Large type books.
  I. Title.
PS3553.O55465I59 2004
  813′.54—dc22   2004057178

For the People of the Book

As the Founder/CEO of NAVH, the only national health agency solely devoted to those who, although not totally blind, have an eye disease which could lead to serious visual impairment, I am pleased to recognize Thorndike Press★ as one of the leading publishers in the large print field.

Founded in 1954 in San Francisco to prepare large print textbooks for partially seeing children, NAVH became the pioneer and standard setting agency in the preparation of large type.

Today, those publishers who meet our standards carry the prestigious "Seal of Approval" indicating high quality large print. We are delighted that Thorndike Press is one of the publishers whose titles meet these standards. We are also pleased to recognize the significant contribution Thorndike Press is making in this important and growing field.

Lorraine H. Marchi, L.H.D.
Founder/CEO
NAVH

★ Thorndike Press encompasses the following imprints: Thorndike, Wheeler, Walker and Large Print Press.

There is no such thing as shadow.
Only air deprived of light.

— *LUCRETIUS*
De Rerum Natura

KINGDOM COUNTY, WEST VIRGINIA

SUMMER, 1984

PART 1

CHAPTER ONE

There is no older story than the return of the native, and I'd always believed that had Adam returned to Eden to walk in middle age the ruined garden once again, he might have felt an odd nostalgia for his fall. And yet I felt no such nostalgia for Kingdom County. In fact, after leaving it, I'd never expected to live there again, see the suspicious look in Sheriff Porterfield's eyes each time I'd met him on the streets of Kingdom City. He'd never said a word to me, but I'd guessed his thoughts:

I know you were there.

The old sheriff had been standing on the corner only a few yards away when I'd climbed onto a bus headed for California a few days after the murders. He'd had that same accusatory look in his eyes, but he'd added a knowing grin as the bus pulled away.

I know what you did.

I'd just turned nineteen that year, a boy on his way to college, armed with a scholarship, seeking only to escape a bloody act, build a life far away from Kingdom County and in every way different from the one I'd lived there. If I'd had one determination as I'd taken my seat in the bus that day, it was that I would never again live in Kingdom County, never again endure its poverty and blighted hope, and certainly not the dark suspicions of Sheriff Wallace Porterfield.

But when my father fell ill, I had no choice but move back. With both my mother and my brother Archie gone, there was no one left to care for him. And although I had nothing in common with my father, nor even so much as a tender childhood memory of him, I couldn't let him die alone.

The fact that he was dying was not in doubt. Doc Poole had made that clear as I sat in his office a few days after my return.

"I want to know exactly what his condition is," I said.

Doc Poole leaned back in his chair. "He won't make it through the summer, Roy."

It was a stifling summer afternoon, and even as Doc Poole spoke, the two of us facing each other across his old wooden desk, I knew that a few miles away my father had already retired to his sweltering bedroom, its door sternly closed, as it always had been, my father secluded not only within that steaming space but within himself as well, a chamber just as airless and overheated as the room in which he lay.

"In the last stage of liver cancer there's really nothing to be done," Doc Poole added. "So I wouldn't waste any time on false hope."

"I never have," I said casually.

"What did Jesse tell you about his situation?"

"Just that he had cancer. He didn't say he was in the last stage of anything. He didn't even ask me to come home."

"Well, I'm glad you did," Doc Poole told me. "You can help him stay comfortable."

"I'll do what I can," I said crisply.

Keep him comfortable, that was my sole purpose in coming home, simply to care for my father's most immediate needs, nothing more. I had not come home to reconcile with him, win his approval, or confess anything. As far as I was concerned my father was a crude and ignorant man who took a bullish pride in his crudity and ignorance, wore them like badges of honor. So much so that he often seemed determined to offend me, forever sprawled in his musty, littered bedroom, wearing nothing but boxer shorts and a sleeveless undershirt, his legs spread wide, a cigarette burning down to the nub in his soiled fingers. At dinner he wiped his mouth with the back of his hand and noisily gulped the last swallow of iced tea, defiantly staring at me when he set down the glass. Day and night, he watched one mindless TV comedy after another, seemingly as amused by the commercials as by the programs themselves. Even in sleep he seemed bent upon disturbing me, twisting about violently as he muttered my brother's name, *Archie, Archie,* as if to make it clear that my dead brother was the one he would have preferred beside him in his last days.

I might have attributed all of this spitefulness to the simple fact that my father was dying and, therefore, unhappy. But he'd always been unhappy. I couldn't remember a time when a rancorous misery hadn't afflicted him. Nor did it surprise me that in his final weeks on earth this unquiet ghost continued to goad him mercilessly, giving no quarter, determined to pursue him to the grave. There were even times when I thought I could hear it hissing through the air around him, a voice as dry as the sound of wind through fields of long-dead corn.

The origin of my father's unhappiness remained a mystery, however. He'd never spoken of his life, nor offered me the slightest entry into his shrouded past. And so I'd finally concluded that his unhappiness was like my own, something that flowed from the choices I'd made. And although our choices had been complete opposites, they'd landed us pretty much in the same boat. My father had made a bad marriage. I had

16

chosen not to marry. He had sired two sons, and in one way or another, lost them both. I'd had no children. In both our lives, the dream of family had soured, leaving us tied cheerlessly to each other, my father yearning only for death, I yearning only to escape once again from the very place I'd fled so many years before.

But as I realized a few days after returning to Kingdom County, my yearning to escape it was even deeper now, a need, once and for all, to put its gory legacy behind me. For by then I'd learned how violence clings to whatever it touches. You can wash the blood away but not the memory of blood, not whose it was or how it had been spilled. Innocence is fragile, and violence shatters it. A simple pair of scissors once tagged Exhibit A can never cut kite string again.

The merest glance into my childhood bedroom, the sight of Archie's battered guitar still propped up in the corner, could instantly evoke the sound of gunfire, clouds of blue smoke.

My brother and I had shared that tiny room from earliest boyhood until his last night at home. We had crammed it with big plans, usually of escape, first to Kingdom City and from there to parts unknown. It was in that room I'd first determined to go to college, then later filled out the necessary application. I'd read the letter of acceptance, one that had been accompanied by the offer of a scholarship, in a kind of wild reverie, leaping onto the bed and jumping up and down while Archie looked on silently.

It was also in that room that Archie had first mentioned Gloria, and where, sometime later, he'd told me that he was in love with her. Later still, he'd mused about how the two of them would one day get married, move to Nashville, find an apartment, attend the Grand Ole Opry every Saturday night. The little metal box he'd used as a bank still rested on the small wooden table by the window. I could hear the soft tinkle of coins as he counted out his savings each night, trying to calculate, in that confused and uncertain way of his, just how much money they would need to get to Nashville and survive there until he made it as a country singer.

But for all the big talk, the plan had remained fuzzy, the money scant, so that I'd never taken it seriously, nor felt any real alarm. And yet, in the end, he'd done it, or at least tried to do it, trudging from the house on a snowy December night, prowling the roads for hours, relentlessly screwing up his courage before finally pulling up beside the tall, dark hedge at 1411 County Road. Even when I imagined all that had happened after that, I made sure to keep it at a distance, like something seen from a great height. Only the mailbox returned to me as it had actually appeared that night, decked with plastic holly, green leaves, and small red berries, snow still half obscuring the family name that had been painted so ornately on its black metal side.

As for Archie, I most often saw him as a boy, eternally clothed in jeans and a white T-shirt, strumming his guitar and crooning country songs. In memory, he was everywhere. Sitting on the steps of the porch or at the kitchen table. Sometimes I glimpsed him on his bed, sitting in his underwear, idly flipping through a comic book. At other times I recalled him at seventeen, standing at the rear door, peering out into our littered backyard, his hands sunk into the pockets of his jeans, thinking no doubt of Gloria, love like a whip snapping in his mind.

I saw my dead mother in the old house too, but always as a figure crouched beside her bed, bare knees on the bare floor, hands clasped before tightly closed eyes, dreaming of a cup that could be passed, sins that could be forgiven, the salvation of good thieves.

But now, in the house where my mother died, I saw only reminders of what could not be undone. The little drawer where my father had kept his pistol. The cheap plastic frame that had once held Gloria's picture. Archie's baseball bat propped up against my father's bed. Scooter's collar nestled among the clutter at the bottom of the closet. Everything bore the mark of our family's affliction, all we'd run from, spread, the things we'd suffered and the suffering we'd caused.

And so, even during these last days of my father's life, I found myself fleeing him and the house he'd hated but never left, darting from it at every opportunity just as I had when I was a boy.

That boy seemed even further from me now than my mother or Archie. I never envisioned him in my old room, never saw him sitting reading a book on the orange sofa, dreaming of college, of moving "up north" or "out west," becoming a teacher, having a wife and children, finding a simple happiness. If I thought of him at all, it was as the ten-year-old child who'd once drawn Archie into a scheme of escape, repeatedly hammered at him about how easily we could do it — *We could leave at night, get to Saddle Rock, sleep there till morning, then go on to Kingdom City, hop a train from there* — so that I'd finally convinced him to join me in the effort.

That dream of escape was the one hope I'd realized from my boyhood. And so, for the last twenty years I'd lived in a small town in northern California, where I taught English at a little boarding school that rested, jewel-like, by the sea. In that idyllic world I taught Chaucer and Shakespeare to the state's most privileged sons and daughters, "snot-nosed rich kids" according to my father, but whom I labored to invest with the refinements my own childhood had so sorely lacked.

I'd visited my father only rarely since moving to California, usually around Christmas, when my own loneliness overwhelmed me and any family connection seemed better than none. Once we'd actually erected a scrawny Christmas tree, strung it with a few colored lights and wads of tinsel. It had still been standing, dry and brown, when I'd returned the following spring. That was when I'd realized how desperately my father was waiting to die.

The sense of welcomed death curled all around him now, a white mist that seemed to boil up from the smoldering center of all that had gone wrong, the wife he'd never loved, the son who'd died, and me.

It was in order to flee that mist that I often left the house and drove into Cantwell, the tiny hamlet close to our house. It was little more than a few dilapidated stores set on a rural crossroads, but a place where I could linger for a time, if only on the pretext of buying supplies. "I have to pick up a few things, Dad," I'd say, then rush out the door, returning later with a cabbage or a box of cereal, ready to hear my father's usual rebuke, *You went all the way into Cantwell for no more'n that?*

But on that particular afternoon — the one

that changed everything — I made no excuse for leaving my father.

I popped my head just inside his room, sniffed the Vicks VapoRub he habitually smeared across his chest and shoulders, and said simply, "I'm going out, Dad."

He gave no indication that he'd heard me, but merely sat, motionless as a granite headstone before the flickering light of the television.

He'd thrown open the room's unwashed curtains, and beyond the window a blinding summer light fell over a parched yard where bedraggled clumps of crabgrass withered in the heat.

"You need anything before I go?" I asked.

He continued to stare at the television I'd lugged into his room a few days before, watching as one wrestler slammed another to the mat.

"It's all fake, you know," I said.

"What ain't?" my father replied with a wave of his hand. "Stay gone as long as you want, Roy. I don't need you."

Never had and never would, he meant.

"I'll be back in an hour or so," I told him.

Once outside, I drew a deep restorative breath, let my face bake in the gleaming sunlight as if light and heat might be sufficient to burn away the toxic residue left by my father, along with the memory of those final sullen evenings when we'd sat in stony silence, Archie dead, my mother curled up in her bed, me set to leave for a California college in only a few days, certain that once I'd left I would miss no one but my mountain girl, return to Kingdom County only to marry her, then take both of us out of it again, out of it forever without so much as a backward glance.

Inside the house I could hear the drone of the television, the thud of heavy muscular bodies hitting the mat, the high, hysterical voice of the announcer calling out the holds, the blows.

When I reached the car, I looked back toward the house. A gray light flickered in the old man's room, faint as whatever dream of happiness he might once have had. As for me, I had only one dream left. To be through with this last remnant of my family, and with him the bloody act with which our name had so long been joined.

CHAPTER TWO

I had no particular destination in mind when I backed my car out of the driveway that morning. Very little had changed in the look and feel of Kingdom County since I'd left it. It was still crisscrossed by narrow, unpaved roads, dotted with small placid ponds, a rural world where only the occasional tipple of a coal mine gave any suggestion of modern industry. The woods were lush and green, and sunlight sparkled on the slender creeks that twisted through them. The air smelled of mountain laurel and honeysuckle, and children still picked blackberries as Archie and I had done as boys, lugging them back to our mother in a metal bucket lined with burlap.

Don't say nothing, Roy. A quick wink. *I'll see you in the blackberry patch.* Those had been Archie's last words to me, uttered as I'd reached the door of his prison cell.

Since that night I'd added other details I may or may not actually have noticed at the time, the play of Archie's fingers in his lap, the shadow of the bars across his face, the plain white T-shirt beneath the orange jailhouse jumpsuit. Still, more than anything, it was his voice I remembered, quiet, calm, assuring me that somehow, in some other world, all the murderous terror of that snowy night on County Road would be put behind us.

He's like a little puppy, Roy, so you have to keep an eye on him, my mother used to say. *So he don't run in front of a car or just trot off with a stranger.*

Even as a boy I'd recognized Archie's guileless nature and lack of foresight. I'd been so much the leader of our small pack that at times he'd seemed paralyzed without me. My father had stated the fact of the matter with his typical brutality: *Murder was the only thing that boy ever done without you, Roy,* a line that burned into my mind each time my father said it, made me see again the headlights of my old Chevy mount the hill at 1411 County Road, glint on the rear bumper of Archie's black Ford as it rested beside the high green hedge, Archie hunched behind the wheel, tense, baffled, poised to act, but unable to do so, his question whispering always in my mind, *Will you come with me, Roy?*

I still knew a great many people in the area around Cantwell, of course, but the first person I recognized as I drove around that morning was Lonnie Porterfield, the son of the old sheriff who'd presided over Kingdom County like a medieval lord.

We'd been acquaintances in high school,

Lonnie and I, then gone our separate ways, he for a tour in Vietnam, where he'd been wounded seriously enough to win a Purple Heart, then returned home the county's conquering hero.

A few years after his return, Wallace Porterfield had retired as sheriff of Kingdom County with the clear understanding that Lonnie, who'd worked as his deputy until then, would take over the job. Even so, an election was necessary, and during the campaign Lonnie had used his military service to good advantage, run for the office as much on his war record as on whatever experience he'd gained working for the old sheriff. He'd been elected by a wide margin and had held the job ever since.

Normally, I wouldn't have stopped at Lonnie's house, but after three dreary weeks back in Kingdom County, the prospect of talking to someone other than my father — if our tense exchanges could be called talk at all — was too enticing to resist.

Lonnie was leaning back in a lawn chair in his front yard, when I pulled into his driveway. His black-and-white cruiser sat in the front yard, gleaming in the sunlight. A golden five-pointed star adorned the side doors.

"Roy Slater, well, I'll be damned," Lonnie said as I got out of my car. "I heard you were back in town."

I noticed a red plastic bucket beside his chair, suds boiling up over the rim, a wet rag hung over the side.

"Washing the car on Sunday," I scolded. "Isn't there a law against that in Kingdom County?"

"I'm the law in Kingdom County," Lonnie said, using the very words he'd no doubt heard his father say a thousand times. "Besides, Sunday's the only time I got to do it. How long you been back, Roy?"

"Couple of weeks."

"Have a seat. As you can see, I'm taking a break."

I dropped into the chair beside him. "I can't stay long."

"I heard your daddy wasn't doing too good."

"He's still able to get around, but I don't know how much longer that will last. Doc Poole gave him about three months, but that was some time back. He has less now."

"Hard thing, watching your daddy die," Lonnie said.

I nodded, though it struck me as more inconvenient than hard.

"I dread facing it," Lonnie added, then chuckled. "Of course, my old man's just about indestructible."

The image of Wallace Porterfield rose into my mind, his massive figure forever poised outside my brother's cell, staring down at

Archie as if he were a bug he could, at will, either squash or spare.

Lonnie cooled himself with a cardboard fan emblazoned with a picture of the Lawson Funeral Home, Kingdom City, W.V. "Hot as hell today. Bet you spent the morning like me, under that big shade tree in your front yard."

"It's not there anymore," I said. "My father cut it down."

"When?"

"Few years ago. He said it blocked his view."

"Of what?"

I shrugged.

"That doesn't make much sense, Roy. Why does he do things like that?"

"I don't know. Maybe he just likes destroying things."

"He's a pisser, your old man," Lonnie said with a short laugh. "You'll miss him."

The lie came effortlessly. "Yeah."

Lonnie had quickly gone on to other subjects, and we'd been idly talking politics a few minutes later when Ezra Loggins pulled up in a dusty pickup.

"Morning, Sheriff," Ezra said as he got out of his truck.

Lonnie nodded.

Ezra yanked a baseball cap from his head and raked back his long brown hair as he lumbered toward us. "I come up on something I think you ought to know about, Sheriff."

"What's that?"

Ezra balled the cap up in his large hands. "A body. Up near Jessup Creek."

Lonnie's eyes cut over to me. Then back to Ezra. "So, tell me more."

"Well, I went over to it, of course. But the way it was fixed, I couldn't see much. The face was pressed into the dirt. Couldn't make out a thing 'cept it's a man. I could tell that much from the clothes and the hair cut short. That's all I can say." He shrugged. "Looked like he maybe keeled over dead right there by the creek."

"Was it an old man?" Lonnie asked.

"Didn't look all that old. Didn't notice no white hair or nothing."

"See anybody else around?"

"Not a soul, far as I could tell."

Lonnie leaned forward, thinking, rubbing his hands together. "You didn't touch the body, did you, Ezra?" he asked.

"Nope."

Lonnie got to his feet. "All right. Let's go see about it." He looked at me. "Want to come along, Roy?"

It hadn't occurred to me that Lonnie would ask, but anything seemed better than an early return to my father's house, the thud of wrestlers on the mat, the smell of Vicks.

"When will we be back?" I asked.

"Why, you got something pressing?"

I'd told my father that I'd be back soon, but I recalled the way he'd dismissed my leaving.

"No, I don't have any reason to get back right away," I said.

Lonnie waved me forward. "Let's go, then."

We'd already started for the car when the screen door of the house screeched.

"Where you going, boy?"

He stood in the doorway like a huge gray stone, Wallace Porterfield in all his forbidding majesty.

As a child I'd seen him often, usually outside the sheriff's office, his right hand resting on a pearl-handled pistol. He'd worn a large black hat in those days, with a white band and a small red feather. No man had ever looked more in command of other men. But it was only after the murders that I'd felt the heavy hand of Sheriff Porterfield's presence in Kingdom County, the weight of his eyes as they followed me down the corridor to the cell that imprisoned my brother. More than twenty years had passed since then, but I had little doubt that the old sheriff still remembered Archie sitting dazed in his old Ford, a world of carnage behind the white polished door of the house on the hill above him.

"You finish washing the car, Lonnie?" he asked gruffly.

Lonnie seemed almost to shrink before his father's towering figure, wither beneath the hard light of his relentless gaze. "I didn't quite finish it," he said.

"When you planning to do it, then?"

"When I get back," Lonnie replied.

Wallace Porterfield stepped onto the porch. The boards creaked softly beneath his weight. His hair had gone entirely white. It was cut short and stood on end, the crowning glory of a body that seemed to erupt, dark and volcanic, from the earth. "People don't respect a lawman that drives a dirty car."

"I know," Lonnie answered. "But I've got to attend to something."

"What?"

"Some kind of trouble up around Waylord."

Porterfield laughed, but there was no mirth in his laughter. "Hell, there's always trouble in Waylord."

"Looks like a fellow dropped dead over round Jessup Creek."

Porterfield's eyes suddenly cut over to me. "Do I know you?"

"Roy Slater," I told him.

He said nothing, but I could see the grim pictures playing in his mind, a body tumbling down a flight of stairs, another curled into a corner.

"You arrested my brother, Archie," I said.

As he turned back to Lonnie, he gave no

hint that he'd ever heard of my brother. "You better plan on getting back before sundown. We ain't popular up there in the hills."

Not popular, no. In fact, I doubted that there'd ever been a man more hated by the people who occupied the hills surrounding Kingdom City. He'd ruled by terror and was said to have pocketed large sums given him by the mine owners or their agents, though it was hard for me to see where all that money could have gone, save into the large house he'd built about a mile from Cantwell.

Porterfield glanced at me again, as he might have glanced at a bird on a limb. Then he eased his enormous frame back toward the house. At the door he stopped, his huge head rotating on the thick folds of his neck until he looked me square in the eye. "You going up there too?" he asked.

I nodded.

He appeared indifferent to whether I went or stayed.

"Take a shotgun," he said, returning his attention to Lonnie. "Nothing stops a man like a shotgun."

CHAPTER THREE

Waylord was a whorl of hills and gaps that lay in the far northeastern corner of Kingdom County. As a boy, I'd known it only as a remote and mysterious place where there was no electricity, no phones, no radios, nor much of anything else that couldn't have been found in the same houses a hundred years before. The people who lived there drew water from wells, cooked on woodstoves, washed their clothes in the same metal tubs they used to bathe their children and themselves. In summer the women wore broad, bright-colored bonnets to shield their faces from the sun, tended their gardens in dresses made from feed sacks or bolts of cloth chosen from mail order catalogues.

My father had come from Waylord, and so, all my life, I'd thought of it as a primitive place, rocked by bloody feuds and mining wars, peopled by a race of Highland warriors whose fallen progeny now dug out a living from the hardscrabble soil, fished, hunted, made their own whiskey, and sometimes their own laws.

And yet, despite the deep roots his family had sunk in Waylord, my father had never spoken of it fondly. In fact, his opinion of it had differed little from Wallace Porterfield's. "Nothing worth a damn up there," he'd say at first mention of the place, then quickly go on to another, less bitter subject.

But while my father appeared genuinely hostile to Waylord, Lonnie was merely irritated by it.

"I'll have to wash the whole car over again, dammit," he muttered as we swung off the main road and onto the unpaved one that led up to Ezra Loggins's farm. He eyed the film of dust that had already begun to gather on the hood and shook his head. "I try my best to stay out the hills. But just like Daddy says, these damn people up here are always getting into something." He glanced out over the withered fields. "If you ask me, good sense stops at Bishop's Gap. After that, pure craziness takes over."

It took forty minutes of plowing through the thick undergrowth, circling around patches of poison oak and brier bushes, slapping at gnats and plucking thorns from our trousers as we walked, before we finally reached the body. And yet, for all the difficulty of the trip, it was the wildflowers I noticed, swirls of white and red that brought back a sweeter time of life, years when things had seemed easier than they did now, the route to happiness less plagued by pits and snares. A voice returned to me, though I scarcely dared give it a face, *We're going to make it, aren't we, Roy.*

"There it is." Ezra pointed to a mound in the distance. A shallow culvert lay just beyond it, Jessup Creek ran through it. "Looks like a pile of rags, don't it, Sheriff? Just like I said."

The corpse lay curled over, knees folded beneath the trunk, buttocks raised, so that it looked as if it had simply tumbled headfirst off the stump just behind it. Dappled sunlight played on a blue flannel shirt. The jeans had the faded look of old denim, the soles of the brown leather boots were cracked and dusty.

"You notice the gun before?" Lonnie pointed to a single-shot twenty-two rifle that lay, half covered with leaves, a few feet from the body.

Ezra shook his head. "I didn't look at things too close."

Lonnie circled the dead man, studying the ground. He stopped to gather other things Ezra hadn't noticed: a box of cartridges, several empty casings. Something else caught his eye. He lifted the head from the ground. A gummy swath of blood covered the face.

"Damned if I can tell who it is," he said as he let the head fall forward again.

A wallet bulged from the back pocket of the dead man's jeans. Lonnie pulled it out, flipped it open, took out the driver's license. "Clayton Spivey."

"Who's Clayton Spivey?" I asked.

"Ah, just some guy lives up here," Lonnie said. He looked at Ezra. "How does he make do anyway?"

Ezra shrugged.

"Does he make whiskey?"

"I don't think so, Sheriff."

"Where does he live exactly?"

Ezra nodded toward the woods that stretched northward along the creek. "Up that way, I think. About three miles."

"Three miles," Lonnie repeated. His eyes shifted over to me. "Well, that ought to make it interesting for you, Roy."

"For me?" I asked. "Why?"

He looked at me wonderingly. "Well, think about it. Three miles up Jessup Creek. You know what that means, don't you?"

"No."

"Well hell, Roy, that means old Clayton here was living on Lila Cutler's land," Lonnie said. He winked at Ezra. "Roy may not know much about old Clayton here," he added with a quick grin. "But he sure as hell knows plenty about Lila Cutler. Am I right, Roy? You know about Lila, don't you?"

Her face swept toward me through a bright summer afternoon, her hair glistening, wet and free in the cool stream water as she swam toward me.

"I know a little," I said.

"A little?" Lonnie laughed. "If all you know's

36

a little, you ain't the man I thought you was." He peered about, taking in the thick green woods. "Fine-looking girl, Lila was."

Her hair flowed down her back as she swam toward me, long white legs slicing through the blue water.

"Graduated from Waylord High," Lonnie told Ezra. He drew a pocket knife from Spivey's jeans. "Probably the first Cutler that ever finished school, don't you guess, Roy?"

She smiled brightly, the face now poised triumphant beneath the mortarboard as she flicked its gold tassel to the right.

"The very first," I told him.

Lonnie stood up, slapped forest debris from the knees of his trousers. "Lila Cutler. Fine-looking girl." He looked at Ezra.

"There's an old mining road not too far from here, right, Ezra?"

Ezra's eyes were on Clayton Spivey. "Yeah, there is," he answered. "It used to come all the way from the Waylord mine."

"My guess is Clayton came right down that road." Lonnie thought a moment, then added, "Probably walked right through the pasture behind the Cutler place. Unless he had a car. Did Clayton have a car, Ezra?"

"I think his car was broke down, Sheriff."

"Why you think that?"

" 'Cause I seen him walking back and forth a few times. On foot, I mean. Going down the mountain."

Lonnie shrugged. "Well, I'll go check his place soon as I finish up here," he said, the professional lawman plotting the course of his investigation. He glanced down at the corpse. "Clayton Spivey lived like a hermit, didn't he? No wife or kids."

"Far as I know he lived alone."

Lonnie laughed. "Just like old Roy here, living the bachelor's life. Hell, I can't even remember not being married, can you, Ezra? Not having a wife and kids?"

I felt a curious emptiness settle upon me as Lonnie and Ezra chuckled together, married men, men with children.

"Did Lila ever get married?" I asked quietly.

Lonnie looked surprised by the question. "Man, you really haven't kept in touch with the old home place, have you, Roy?"

"No, I haven't."

"Well, no, Lila never got married," Lonnie answered. "She's still living with her mother in that same old house they lived in when Lila was a girl."

For a moment, the girl Lila had once been seemed to rise into Lonnie's mind. Then, no less suddenly, it vanished, and he glanced down again at Clayton Spivey's body.

"Well, now I got to find out what happened to this poor bastard," he said.

It was midday by the time an ambulance from the county hospital arrived at Ezra

Loggins's farmhouse. I didn't go back into the woods, felt no need to see Clayton's body again. And so I stayed behind while Lonnie and Ezra led the ambulance attendants back up into the hills. Two hours passed before they showed up again, clumsily bearing a stretcher from the edge of the woods to the back of the ambulance.

"Walked over to Clayton's place," Lonnie said as he trudged toward me. "Nothing but a shack. Just a little table and a chair. An old woodstove." He shook his head disdainfully. "Living like an animal."

"He was poor," I said.

Lonnie appeared hardly to have heard me. "Still can't tell what happened to him. Rifle didn't have any blood on it, but somebody could have wiped it clean."

"You think he was shot?"

"Can't tell that either," Lonnie answered. "At least not without a real close look. With that little old peashooter he had, he could have got shot and you wouldn't even find the hole without shaving his head. Happened to a guy in Welch. Got shot twice in the head, and nobody found the holes till the doctor took a look at him in the emergency room."

"What about suicide?" I asked.

Lonnie shrugged. "Same story. If Clayton put that gun in his mouth and pulled the trigger, you wouldn't see no hole on the other side."

"But you'd see blood on the barrel, wouldn't you?"

Lonnie grinned, pleased. "You're a regular detective."

"I've read a few detective stories," I said.

"Well, the answer's no, you wouldn't necessarily see any blood. Depends on how long that old rifle was out in the open. Could have been washed by rain, something like that. Fact is, we won't know anything for sure until the coroner takes a look at the body." He glanced toward the overhanging hills. "Anyway, I figure Clayton must have walked all the way from that shack of his to Jessup Creek. That old Pontiac was sitting there with the hood up. I guess he'd been working on it from time to time." He bent forward, picked a burr from his trousers. "Remember that old Chevy you had, Roy?"

"I remember it."

"And that old Ford of your brother's."

I saw it parked beside the hedge, Archie behind the wheel, looking scared as I pulled up beside him.

"Ratty old thing, Archie's car," Lonnie added. "With those old torn-up seats."

"I didn't realize you ever looked at it that closely," I said.

Lonnie shrugged. "Well, it was parked out behind my daddy's office for quite a while."

Parked for several weeks, I knew, my father refusing even to go to the sheriff's office to reclaim it, determined to let the old Ford rot where it stood rather than do what he had to do to get it back, *I ain't asking Porterfield for that car. You go get it if you want it so bad.*

"Whatever happened to it?" I asked now.

"Daddy give it away, I guess. He sure wouldn't have been caught dead in an old wreck like that. He drives a Lincoln Town Car now. Where'd your daddy find that old wreck anyway?"

"He didn't," I said.

"Your daddy didn't buy it?"

"No, Archie did. He saved up and bought it."

"Worked at the hardware store, didn't he? And you worked at Clark's Drugs in Kingdom City." He slapped dust from the shoulders of his uniform. "Soda jerk."

I nodded. "You have a good memory, Lonnie."

"Got it from my daddy, I guess," Lonnie said. He drew a handkerchief from his back pocket and wiped his face. "Well, now for the hard part." He returned the handkerchief to his pocket. "Got to go up to Lila's place."

"Lila's place? Why?"

"Because Clayton lived on her land. And with him not having any family and all, Lila probably knows as much as anybody about him." He considered the lowering sun. "I figure we can still get back to town before nightfall. That's my plan anyway."

41

We wasted no time on the road that twined upward into the surrounding hills. As we drove, the distance lengthened between farmhouses and the woods thickened until they became as close to a choking tropical jungle as the temperate zone allows.

"When were you up this way last, Roy?" Lonnie asked, one hand on the wheel, the other dangling out the open window.

"Not since I left."

"Back when you were courting Lila?"

"Yeah."

"You were coming up here pretty often in those days, I bet."

I recalled the anticipation of the drive, the long winding road that led to her house. "Pretty often," I answered.

The breeze slapped at Lonnie's short-sleeve shirt. His eyes cut over to me. "Lila your first love?"

Only love, I thought. The one hope I'd had for a wife, children, and which had died the day she wrote me in California, a letter whose final words still echoed in my mind, *I can't be your wife, Roy. Don't come back for me.*

"When was the last time you saw her?" Lonnie asked when I didn't answer.

"The day I left."

"You mean for college?"

"That's right."

"I heard she threw you over. But I never

heard why she did it."

"I never knew either."

Lonnie heard something in my voice, maybe. He said, "There's always one you never get over."

I gave no response, though what Lonnie said was true enough. Not a single day had gone by in the twenty years that had passed since I'd last seen Lila that I hadn't thought of her. I'd angrily tossed out the few pictures I had of her, discarded her letter, thrown away even the slightest memento of the time we'd spent together, and yet she'd haunted me through the years. The sight of a wildflower could bring her back, but I'd glimpsed her, too, at ball games and soda fountains, heard her laugh behind me in a darkened movie theater.

"With me it's Charlotte," Lonnie said. "Charlotte Bethune. You remember her, don't you?"

I did. She'd never raised her hand in class or uttered a single memorable word, but despite all that, Charlotte Bethune had given off the unmistakable scent of ripe sexuality, a red, swollen cherry of a girl.

"Charlotte Bethune," Lonnie repeated, like he could taste her name in his mouth. "Married Randy LaFavor. Moved to Oklahoma. Probably got six kids by now. Probably weighs a ton." He laughed. "The girl a boy dreams of never grows old, never

43

gets fat. She just sits there in your brain, like time couldn't touch her. Perfect."

In my mind I saw us on the old mining road, a young couple, hand in hand, walking slowly in the darkness, thinking only of each other until the first roar of the motor sounded distantly, then the first glimpse of the truck's yellow lights, heading toward us out of the night.

"Must have been tough, losing Lila," Lonnie added after a moment, still the prying teenager I remembered from my youth, still picking for some unseemly detail or hint of injury, the pain of others like honey on his tongue.

When I didn't respond, he turned back toward the road, then thrust the gear into second as we mounted the last remaining hill. "There it is," he said after we'd come over its rounded crest.

Lila's place sat at the edge of a wide pasture, an unpainted farmhouse with a high tin roof, discolored by long runnels of rust. A green tractor with worn wheels was parked beside a large wooden shed, the mud-caked blades of its metal tiller drooping heavily to the ground behind it. A dusty black pickup was parked beside it, nearly treadless tires spattered with mud, the front bumper slumped to the right like a shattered shoulder.

"Looks like things haven't improved much

for Lila." Lonnie pressed on the brake, brought us to a halt in the driveway. He peered at the pasture that swept out from behind the house, goldenrod weaving softly in the breeze. His gaze shifted to the house, taking in its dilapidated state, the rusty tools gathered in a large tub at the bottom of the wooden stairs, the ancient washing machine that sat near the edge of the porch, an oily rag dangling from its hand-cranked wringer. "Lila's sure not living at the top of the pile."

"She never did," I said, recalling how raw her poverty had been, the few home-made dresses she'd had, the single pair of shoes.

Lonnie grabbed the door handle. "You coming?"

"No. I'll wait here."

"You don't want to say hello to your old flame?"

"No."

Lonnie grinned. "Still pissed at her, Roy? Or just afraid to see what time can do?"

From behind the dust-smeared windshield, I watched as Lonnie strode across the nearly barren lawn, moving briskly up the wooden stairs, then rapped harshly at the door, as if he'd brought an arrest warrant for Lila rather than news of Clayton Spivey's death.

The door opened, but I couldn't see who opened it, only the suggestion of a slender figure poised at the entrance of the darkened house.

"Hey there, Lila," I heard Lonnie say as he stepped inside the house, leaving the door open behind him.

Across the pasture, the forest rose in a tangled barricade of green. In the hard white light, an old mule stood, head down, nosing through the high grass. A line of unpainted fence posts stretched the length of the field, strung with drooping strands of rusted wire. At the edge of the yard an orange tabby hunkered down, belly low, eyes fixed on the small sparrow that hopped obliviously a yard away.

Even now, after having been away from it for so long, I could feel Waylord's heaviness, dense and blinding, a pull of the earth that grounded everything, turned the most feathery wings into sheets of lead. It didn't surprise me that even Lila, for all her spirit and determination, had finally been held in place by the iron grip of these hills. Escape for a man had been hard enough, but for a woman, it was impossible.

The slap of a screen door brought my gaze back to the house.

Lonnie was on the porch. Through the screen, the woman behind it was no more than a hint of white behind rusty brown filament.

After a moment he nodded silently, then strode down the stairs and walked swiftly toward the car, his gait bearing no sign of the dark news he'd just delivered.

"Well, that's done," he said as he pulled himself behind the wheel, hit the ignition, and thumped the car into reverse. "Didn't say much. Not much of a talker, Lila."

I glanced toward the house. Lila no longer stood behind the screen.

"I told her that we'd take Clayton's body down to the funeral home in Kingdom City," Lonnie said as we angled back onto the road. "She said she'd come down and identify the body. You know, officially." He pressed down on the accelerator, and the shack drifted back like a small boat on a deep green tide. "Didn't see her mama. I guess her health's failing."

A small, round woman, as I recalled her, curiously voluptuous, though in her forties she had seemed ancient to me at the time.

We were moving down the road now, jostling along its narrow ruts.

"As for Lila, she just stood there with her arms folded," Lonnie said. "You know how she is. Can't get more than a one-word answer out of that girl."

Her voice raced through my mind, fervent, full of spirit, certain that with her the cycle would be broken, all the poverty and blighted hope of those who'd come before her. *I'm going to find a way out of Waylord, Roy. You need to find one too.*

Until then, I thought I had.

(HAPTER FOUR

My father was sitting in his bed when I got back to the house, his hair in its usual disarray, the bed's one sheet wadded up and hurled into a corner.

"Where you been, Roy?" he asked sharply.

"With Lonnie Porterfield."

"What business you got with him?"

"I don't have any business with him. I just paid a visit."

"Mighty long visit."

"We got caught up in something."

"His wife left him, you know." My father said it with satisfaction. "Ain't no woman had nothing to do with him since then."

My father's pleasure at Lonnie's failed marriage struck me as purely malicious, as if his own unhappy marriage could find comfort only in the knowledge that other marriages had been no less stricken.

"Probably didn't give a damn about him by the time she left," my father added. "Probably raised his hand to her and that's why she left him."

"What makes you think that?"

" 'Cause that's the way they are, them Porterfields." Before I could respond, he added,

"Got a skinny little daughter that works at the Crispy Cone. Wild as hell, I heard."

"Who tells you all this, Dad?"

He appeared to resent the question. "I keep track of things."

"The Porterfields in particular, it seems."

"What do you care who I keep track of?"

"I don't, but —"

"Just people in books, them's the only ones you take an interest in."

I picked up the sheet, began folding it. "You have any preference for supper?"

"Preference," my father said, as if the word were too fancy to be uttered in his presence, lay like a silk shirt on his rough back. He plucked a magazine from the table beside his bed, the tattered remnant of something called *Boxing News*. "Just a glass of lemonade."

For a moment, I peered at him wonderingly, as I had when I was a boy, still vaguely yearning to uncover that part of him that remained deep and unfathomable, and yet sometimes broke the surface, like the black fin of a shark.

He glanced up from the page. "What is it?" he barked, looking me dead in the eye.

I shook my head. "Nothing."

He returned to his magazine. "Put lots of ice in that lemonade," he snapped. "And lots of sugar." With that he rolled onto his side, purposely giving me his back.

I went to the kitchen, pulled out one of

the old jelly jars my mother had used for glasses, this one painted with bright red cherries. She'd called it her "collection," and pretended it had value, when, in fact, it had served only to demonstrate how little we'd had, "collections" of plates, twine, tinfoil, paper bags, a bounty of want and scarcity.

Most of what she'd gathered together had been lost since her death, so that now the old wooden cabinet contained only a few glasses and a short stack of chipped plates. Drawers that had once overflowed with matchbooks, buttons, rubber bands, were now very nearly empty. As for her clothes, my father had burned them in a ragged pile the day after her funeral, poking it idly with a stick as the stinking smoke curled upward into a washed-out sky.

I took the old pitcher my grandmother had given her as a wedding gift, mixed water, sugar, bottled lemon juice, then plucked an ice tray from the refrigerator, held it under running water, tapped the cubes into the pitcher.

My father now sat Indian-style, staring out the window, spidery blue veins on naked legs so white they seemed never to have been touched by sun.

"Here's your lemonade," I told him.

"You put in plenty of sugar?"

"Until the water wouldn't dissolve any more."

He took the glass, raised it above his head, studied the layer of white granules that rested at its bottom, then took a long swig, tucked the glass between his legs, and glanced toward the window again. "You sure you want to stay till the end, Roy? Till I'm dead."

"I told you I would."

He took another swig of lemonade, his eyes following the flight of a crow over the pasture. "You don't have to."

"I know I don't."

He took another sip, lowered the glass into his lap. "Sometime before fall, then. That ain't long, is it?"

"No, it's not."

"I heard somewhere that a bug lives about a month." He laughed, his yellow teeth showing briefly, several chipped and crooked, treated with the same indifference with which he'd treated everything else. "I got about the same time as a bug, right, Roy?"

"I wouldn't know."

He looked at me irritably. "That the way you answer them schoolkids you teach? Can't just say 'I don't know.' Got to say it fancy. 'I wouldn't know.'"

"It's just a way of speaking, Dad."

"Teacher talk, that's what it is."

He'd always been contemptuous of my work, considered it fit only for old maids, my being a teacher offering yet more evidence that there was something missing in me, the main part of a man. He'd never encouraged my early ambition to go to college, nor taken any pride in the fact that I'd finally gotten a degree. But now he seemed at war with everything I had become since leaving Waylord, not only my choice of career, the fact that I lived on the other side of the country, but with my grammar, my vocabulary, everything.

But I also knew that something else was going on in him, old demons clawing at his mind, my "fancy" language merely the grappling hook that had dragged something more unsettling from the swamp.

He drained the last of the lemonade and shoved the empty glass toward me. "Anyway, when it comes to dying, I'd rather go like a bug. Not thinking about it." His eyes drifted toward the old ball bat that rested at a slant against his bed and which he'd begun to use to lift himself from the bed. "One thing's for damn sure," he said, now fingering its handle, "you won't see me go out like Archie done."

So that was it, I thought. He was thinking about Archie, his life and death pressing like a red-hot iron against his flesh.

"Crack like Archie done. Pissing and moaning."

In an instant, I recalled my brother during the only time my father had gone to see him in the county jail. He'd been taken completely unaware by the seizure that had left

Archie balled up and whimpering on the concrete floor of his cell, my father nudging him with his boot, demanding that he get up, his eyes whipping back and forth from Archie's crumpled body to where Wallace Porterfield stood just outside the bars, arms folded over his huge chest, a look of absolute contempt in his eyes.

"Shaking all over," my father muttered. His mouth took a cruel twist. "Life ain't worth it. If I could turn it off, just like that light switch there, I'd do it right now. It don't mean a thing to me."

"It's different when you're young. When you have some life left."

His eyes slashed over to me. "What do you mean by that?"

"I mean that Archie wasn't like you, Dad. He wasn't ready to die. It's different when you're young."

"No, it ain't," my father snapped. "It ain't no different at all. It don't matter, young or old. You're the same man facing it all the way through. You know why? 'Cause a man don't never change. Take you, Roy. You ain't changed one bit since you was a kid. You still got that same look on your face. Looking down your nose. At everything. This here place. Me."

"I don't look down my nose at you, Dad."

My father laughed. "Oh, you're nice about it. You don't say nothing. But I can see it,

Roy. What you really think. That I'm just some old ignorant bastard from the hills. But let me tell you something, they's things I know that you ain't got no idea about. Things you believe that I ain't never believed. Stupid things."

"Like what?"

He started to blurt out something, then held it back.

"Like what?" I said again.

"Like no matter how much you got, they ain't nothing to it if you ain't got nobody along with you."

I had no doubt as to where this was going, another assault upon my failure to produce a family, even one as doomed and miserable as his own.

"I live alone because I want to," I said, then got to my feet. I was halfway to the door when he drew me back with a question.

"What was it, by the way? That thing you got caught up in this afternoon. With Lonnie Porterfield."

"I went up to Waylord with him."

"Waylord?" The very mention of the place appeared to fill my father with revulsion. "What'd you go up there for? There ain't nothing up there but bad luck."

"Somebody found a body along Jessup Creek. I happened to be over at Lonnie's when he heard about it. So I went along with him. Just for the ride, you might say."

He thumped a cigarette from the pack by his bed. "Whose body was it?"

"Clayton Spivey."

He said nothing, but I could see that he recognized the name.

"After that we drove up to Lila Cutler's place," I added. "You remember Lila, don't you?"

"'Course I remember Lila. She was the only girl you ever brought home."

I saw her as she'd come toward him that night, my father rising to greet her, offering his hand, taking hers gently into his, a strange tenderness in his eyes, as if, at that moment, he'd striven to be some other man he'd failed to be.

"For a while it looked like you was gonna marry Lila," my father added. "Have kids. Maybe have a normal life. A family."

"I'm glad you had such high hopes for me, Dad," I said.

"A family," my father repeated, his eyes on the charred tip of the match. "Not like it turned out."

"My life's really not so bad," I told him.

He seemed amazed that I could come to such a conclusion.

"But you ain't got nobody, Roy," he said. "No wife. No kids of your own. You can't say that's normal, can you?"

"It's the way I want it."

"But why would you want that? Living alone. With nobody."

"It's my life. Drop it."

"But why would you want a life like that? No family, I mean."

I stared him in the eye. "Maybe because of what my life was like when I *had* a family."

My father's face jerked into a scowl. "Oh shit, you're not going to start whining about all that again, are you, Roy?"

"We weren't happy, Dad. Archie. Mama. None of us was happy."

"Whining, whining. Goddamn, Roy. Why don't you just get in that car of yours and go on back to California?"

"Maybe I will," I said sharply.

Something exploded behind his eyes. "Then do," he snarled. "You don't have to stay here. Hell, no, by God. I never asked you to come and I ain't asked you to stay. You can go on back to that . . . whatever it is. That little room you got. Tend to them little snot-nosed kids that ain't your own." He shook his head disdainfully. "Pitiful, Roy. A pitiful life you got."

I watched him evenly, determined to hold my temper in check. "Try to get this through your head, Dad. My life is none of your business."

He shrugged, and the volcanic outburst that had erupted from him seconds before settled no less abruptly.

"You're right," he said, his tone now oddly broken. "Forget it, Roy. Forget I said anything. Turn that TV on. I don't want to talk no more. It's time for my show. Go read your book or something."

But I remained in place, determined to probe at least some small part of his shadowy ire. "I'd just like to know what you get out of it."

"Get out of what?"

"Out of insulting me the way you do. What have I done to deserve that?"

He released a long, weary breath, so that for a moment I actually thought he might reveal some clue as to why he found me so pitiful. "You know what your problem is, Roy? You can't take a joke. You never could."

He waited, watching me. I knew what he wanted, a fiery return, a dog's angry snarl.

Instead, I simply faced him squarely and told the dreadful truth as far as I knew it. "You don't like me, Dad. You have no respect for me or for what I do for a living or for how my life turned out."

"You talk like a man that's already give up on everything, Roy. That ain't got no fight left in him."

"I left my 'fight' when I left Kingdom County," I replied hotly. "So let's put that subject to rest, shall we?" I turned to leave, but he drew me back.

"Run off and bury your nose in a book," he said. "But it don't change the fact that if you don't fight for nothing, you don't amount to nothing."

I whirled around. "What should I fight for, Dad?"

"That's for you to come to," my father shot back. "But I'll tell you one thing, you don't forget them that done you dirt. Like you done with Lonnie today. That burns my ass, Roy. Paying that snot-nosed little bastard a visit. Christ Almighty, of all the people for you to go visiting. Forgetting what he done that night, what he said."

"For God's sake, he was a kid when that happened. Eighteen. Drunk."

"He knew what he was doing, that boy. And you know that too. Drunk or a kid or whatever, he knew exactly what he was saying."

"It was over twenty years ago, Dad. What difference does it make now? Or even then, for that matter?"

"Then?" my father yelped. "I'll tell you what difference it coulda made then. It coulda been Lila wouldn't never have wrote you that letter if Lonnie hadn't said them things."

"What are you talking about?"

"Maybe she got to figuring How come Roy didn't do nothing about that? How come Roy just let it go?"

"And on that basis threw me over? I don't think so."

"All I know is she could have made a good wife for you, Roy. A normal life."

"All that's over and done with, Dad."

My father cut his eyes toward the blank screen of the television. "Ain't nothing ever over and done with, Roy."

"I'm not going to discuss this any further," I said.

" 'Any further,' " my father imitated. "I ain't gonna discuss this here 'any further.' "

We stared at each other icily for a moment, then he shrugged. "I just thought she could have made a man out of you, that's all."

He'd said this last remark without ire, nor any hint of accusation, and yet I felt his words like small exploding shells.

"Well, she didn't," I said. "And after her I never tried again. End of story."

And with that I slammed out of the room, rushed down the corridor and out into the yard, and drew in a long, cleansing breath. I knew at that moment that if I could have willed my father dead, simply flipped that mythical switch, I would have done it.

But it's a hard thing to wish your father dead. And so, with night steadily falling around me, I found myself listening as he dragged himself about his room, attentive to any sign of distress, any sign that he needed me. I knew I owed him nothing and yet I couldn't stop myself from stealing a look through the window, a glimpse of his emaciated form, the right shoulder hunched, his arm bare in the sleeveless T-shirt, skin loose and flabby now, with nothing left of those rippling muscles that had dug coal and cut wood for over fifty years.

Such was the fate of sons, I thought as I continued to wait out the night, listening to the frail chirp of the crickets and katydids, the air cooling now as I tried to cool, watching mutely as the moon retraced its iron circuit, as tightly controlled as I strove to be, solitary and duty-bound, the man Lila Cutler had not made.

CHAPTER FIVE

A windblown summer rain swept in the next morning. I made coffee in my mother's battered tin percolator. I remembered her at the stove in the early morning, her hair gathered in a bun behind her head, already an old woman, it seemed to me, though she'd not yet reached forty.

Even now, solitary though my life had been, I couldn't imagine the cold depths of my mother's loneliness, the deep isolation of living with a man who did not love her, and never had. I couldn't imagine their courtship, my father as a young blade strutting before her, she the object of his pursuit, though I knew that there must have been such a moment in their lives. In fact, it seemed proof enough of a dry and loveless marriage that I could not imagine that earlier time, but only the spoiled residue of it, swollen and malodorous, a blackened fruit.

By the time I was eight, my father had seemed hardly a husband at all. He often took his evening meal in silence, then strode directly to the living room and sat chain-smoking through the night.

Mornings, he lingered in his bedroom as

long as possible, opening and closing drawers like someone who couldn't decide what to wear, though his wardrobe, if it could be called that, had never consisted of more than a few shirts and three or four pairs of work pants.

He'd never taken breakfast with the rest of us, but only grabbed a mug of coffee as he trudged past the kitchen table, then on through the front door, banging the screen behind him, and out to his pickup.

The groan of its engine, the scratch of the tires as he pulled away, had always been followed by a flood of relief that he was gone, taking the weight of his unhappiness with him like a heavy bag.

I had always been the most fully relieved at my father's departure. More than our mother, and far more than Archie, I'd sensed the explosive charge buried deep within him. Perhaps what I'd felt was the sheer, horrific potential of my father for some sudden, annihilating violence, the fact that each day, each hour, seemed to exhaust him in the containment of it. Even in his silence, perhaps most of all in his silence, I sensed a dreadful peril, so that I often felt a wave of relief wash over me when he finally spoke, especially if his words were harsh. When he called me a sissy if I complained about some chore, marveled that I didn't have to "set down" when I peed, or barked "Get off the rag, Roy" to shut me up, at all those times, no matter how stinging the rebuke, his words always came to me like a stay of execution.

But it wasn't my father's long anger that returned to me most vividly as I resumed my boyhood chores that rainy morning. It was Archie, who had always been so much his opposite, a kind, sweet, gentle boy who'd wanted so little from life and gotten so much less.

While I swept and cleaned, he seemed near me, his schoolbooks held together by a worn leather belt as he headed for the yellow school bus on the road, the very bus on which, one bright September morning, he'd sat down next to a shy, slender girl with long blond hair, a girl who'd smiled at him as no girl ever had before, introduced herself, *Hi, my name is Gloria.*

She'd just entered the high school that autumn and she must have seen Archie, tall and slender in his sixteenth year, as a worldly, experienced boy, one who knew the mysterious ways of Kingdom County High School, a boy bound for a diploma, while most all the others had dropped out of school as soon as the law allowed, and after that assumed the lives of their fathers as timbermen, quarrymen, haulers of pulpwood and scrap metal.

To such encouraging prospects, Archie had added his crooning and guitar picking, neither particularly good, but no doubt wondrous to such a girl as Gloria, sheltered as she had always been, crushed beneath the weight of her father's low regard. "Before Archie saw her," Lila said to me one night, "Gloria was invisible."

But once seen, she rose like a comet in my brother's eyes. For a moment I imagined a different fate than the one that had followed. What if Archie had never met Gloria? Or what if he'd met her but things had never gone so terribly awry? What if, on that snowy night, I had not seen my brother's car parked beside the dark hedge, then pulled up beside it?

"You made coffee yet?" my father called from behind the closed door of his bedroom, his voice like a hook, jerking me back to the present.

I poured the coffee into a mug and took it to him.

He was sitting in a chair covered with a ragged patchwork quilt. His hair shimmered in the morning light, curiously soft against the unforgiving features of his face.

"You hear that dog. Barked all damn night." He took a greedy gulp, wiped his mouth. "Just like that old dog Archie had."

In my mind I saw Scooter tied to a fence post at the edge of the pasture, his long tongue lolling in the morning heat, my father's shadow flowing darkly over the grass,

Archie and I following at his side. *We're going hunting, boys.*

"Gimme my gun," he said now.

"You don't have that gun anymore," I said, remembering the old pistol he'd once had but which I knew must be locked in some storage area now, tagged and marked *Kellogg Murders.*

"Sure I got a gun. Twenty-two rifle. In the closet there. Bought it a few months back. Gimme it."

I didn't move. "What do you want with it?"

"What do you think I want with it? I ain't gonna put up with that barking no more."

I shook my head. "You're not going to kill that dog," I told him flatly.

No more than a month before, my father might well have risen from his chair, pushed me aside, and seized the gun himself. Now he glared at me threateningly, then the threat faded away. "Hell, I don't like to sleep anyway. Waste of time. Your mother was always sleeping. Every chance she got. Sleep, sleep, sleep. Always running to the bedroom. Couldn't face nothing. Especially that business with Archie. Couldn't face that, remember?"

I remembered it well. Toward the end she'd balled up under the covers, her bed little different from her grave.

My father glanced toward the window, let

his gaze linger on the dusty road. "So, what plans you got today, Roy?"

"I don't have any plans."

"Not expecting to get 'caught up' in nothing?"

"Not that I know of."

He gulped the last of the coffee, then thrust the cup toward where I stood beside his bed with such sudden force, I stepped back quickly.

"You act like you seen a rattlesnake." He shook his head. "Jumpy. How come you're always so jumpy, Roy?"

When I gave no answer, he said, "You know, I've been thinking about Lila."

"You're not going to bring that up again, are you?"

"Not what we talked about last night, no. Just that I knowed Lila's brother. The one that died. Named Malcolm. Pale as a sheet most of the time. People called him Puker. 'Cause he was always throwing up. At work. In church. Hell, nobody would sit next to him. TB, people said. TB got him. This was before Lila was born, of course. Speaking of dying, what happened to that man up there? That Spivey feller?"

"I don't know," I answered.

He looked at me doubtfully. "You ain't got no idea at all?"

"There was a gun next to him. And there was blood on his face and mouth."

He suddenly grew very still. "Lila know him?"

"I suppose she did. He lived on her land."

"They wasn't related, was they?"

"Not that I know of."

"Then how come you went up to her house?"

"That was Lonnie's idea."

The mention of his name seemed to fill my father's mind with an odd suspicion. "What'd he say? About going up to Lila's house?"

"Just that Spivey lived alone. On Lila's land and so she —"

"— Must have something to do with that feller being dead."

I shook my head. "Lonnie didn't give any indication of —"

"Snooping after dirt," my father interrupted. "His old man was always up in Waylord doing the same thing. Snooping for dirt on people just like Lonnie's trying to get dirt on Lila."

"Why would Lonnie want to 'get dirt' on Lila?" I asked.

"Them Porterfields don't need a reason to go after somebody."

"He was just doing his job, Dad," I said, eager to drop the subject and thereby side-step the enmity that seemed the very bedrock of my father's life.

"Lonnie's going after Lila," my father said with absolute certainty. "You better go see

Lila. Let her know what Porterfield's up to."

"You don't have any evidence that Lonnie's up to anything," I reminded him.

"Maybe so, Roy, but it wouldn't hurt, you going up to have a word with Lila."

"What's on your mind, Dad? What's this business of me going up to see Lila all about?"

He appeared to search for a lie into which he could retreat but found none, and so perhaps answered with the truth. "I just figured maybe you two could start up again. You'd like to do that, wouldn't you, Roy? I mean, you ain't never really give up on her, have you?"

What had never ceased to amaze me was how right my father could be, how clearly he could see the mark, hit it with a word or look. He had read a thought I'd barely perceived myself, that I'd never wholly given up on Lila. But I'd also learned that fruitless love is just another added ache, and so I'd learned to think of Lila like a character in a book, distant and unreal. In an instant, my father had seen all of that, how carefully I had worked to rid myself of Lila, and how fully I had failed to do it.

"It ain't too late for you or her to . . . get together," he said.

"Yes, it is, Dad. I'm not going to get involved with Lila Cutler. I'm not going to marry her somewhere down the line. I'm

68

going to teach school in California, live alone in a small apartment. That's my future. I know you don't like it, but you might as well accept it."

My father's eyes lowered slightly, and he released a soft breath. "Okay," he said. "I just figured she probably still loved you, that's all. In that way, I mean, that you do just once."

"I'm not sure she ever loved me like that."

"Seemed to," my father said. "From the way she looked at you."

He meant the night I'd brought her to meet him, the only time he'd ever seen us together.

"Bet she cried her eyes out when you left for college," he added now.

"Why can't you let this go, Dad? About Lila and me."

He looked vaguely insulted by my question. "Because I'm your father, and it's my job to make a difference. To maybe say that you don't have to live the way you do, Roy. That maybe it ain't too late for you and Lila to —"

"Why are you so intent on Lila being the one I should marry, the mother of my children, and all that?"

" 'Cause I know she'd be a good one. Wife and mother. Comes from good stock."

"Good stock? She's not a heifer, Dad."

"Don't answer me in that smart way, Roy."

69

"You know the point I'm making."

"Well, here's *my* point," my father said. "I know Lila comes from good folks. 'Cause I knew her mother back in the old days. Betty Cutler. She was the best friend of another girl I knew. Girl I used to squire around a little. Deidre, her name was. Deidre Warren. And, like I said, Betty was her best friend. Always together, them two. People used to say it like it was one name, like they was just one person. 'Here comes Betty-and-Deidre,' they'd say. And sure enough, there they'd be. Betty-and-Deidre out for a stroll. Betty-and-Deidre having ice cream at the company store."

"So this was when you worked at the mine?"

"That's right. Betty was a miner's daughter. A miner I worked with back then. Harry was his name. Big feller. Cussed all the time." His eyes lowered to his hands again, the mangled fingers that he couldn't shape into a fist. "When you started going up to see Lila, I knew who she was. Knew she was Betty Cutler's girl. From good stock, like I said. Salt of the earth." He nursed his thoughts briefly, then added, "I guess this thing with Spivey, him living on Lila's land, I guess that brought it all back. Them old days up in Waylord."

During the long summer of our courtship, he'd never said a single word against Lila.

70

The reason had always seemed obvious to me. Lila was a girl from the hills, from fabled Waylord, a girl whose family name my father had instantly recognized. A pretty girl. A smart, lively girl. From the first glimpse of her, he'd given every evidence of being pleased to see her, even honored by the fact that I'd presented her to him, though even then he might well have guessed why I'd done it. That it had come from my need to show him that I'd won a girl more beautiful than my mother had ever been, a smarter girl, more ambitious. I'd waved Lila like a red cape in my father's face. *Take that,* I'd thought as I'd drawn Lila beneath my arm, *Take that, old man.*

She'd worn a dark green dress that night, her long hair falling to her shoulders. My father had risen from his chair to greet her.

"So you're Lila," he said. He drew the cigarette from the corner of his mouth, slapped a bit of tobacco from his taut belly. "Excuse my appearance. I wasn't expecting Roy to bring nobody by."

"That's okay, Mr. Slater," Lila said gently.

"You're mighty pretty." His gaze was oddly wistful.

"Thank you, sir."

A light burned softly behind his eyes. "Take care of her, Roy. You only get one chance."

"He seemed nice," Lila said later.

Even as she'd uttered the word, I'd seen his shadow like a stain on the grass as he'd handed Archie the pistol, Scooter barking madly now, twisting about, his tail wagging furiously, a memory that had sent a poison through my nerves.

And so I'd told Lila the story of how, several years before, Archie and I had run away, then related the gruesome details of what my father had done about it, the terrible punishment he had devised. "Nice?" I'd repeated starkly at the end of it. "Believe me, Lila, you don't know him."

Nor had I ever known him either, I thought now, watching as he withdrew back into himself, lighting his first cigarette of the day, waving out the match.

"Leave me be now," he said.

I nodded and left the room, and with it the old mystery of my father, the coal-black stone from which he had been formed.

(HAPTER SIX

I was sitting in the living room, trying to close out the steady drone of the television in my father's bedroom while I read one of the books I'd brought with me from California, when the phone rang.

I knew that my father would make no effort to answer it, and so I walked into the living room and answered it myself.

"Morning, Roy."

"Morning, Lonnie."

"Your daddy get through the night okay?"

"Some dog kept him up."

I could tell by Lonnie's voice that he hadn't called to check on my father. Something else was on his mind.

"Listen, Roy," he said, "I'm at my office here in Kingdom City. I got Lila Cutler down here."

I pictured her as she'd looked the last time I'd seen her, in that white dress with the long blue sash, eighteen years old, with dark red hair that hung over her shoulders, a crinkle in her nose when she smiled.

"She's not saying much," Lonnie went on. "Won't tell me anything about Clayton. That's why I'm calling. I thought you might drop by this morning, talk to her a little bit."

Before I could protest, he added, "Look, Roy, I let something slip. To Lila, I mean. When I was talking to her this morning. I let slip that you were back in Kingdom County. When I told her the story about Ezra finding the body, then going up to Jessup Creek. It just slipped out that you happened to come along. And the thing is, it had an effect on her."

"Lonnie, I —"

"No harm in you coming by, right? Talking to her?"

I could have gotten out of it, simply told Lonnie that too much time had passed, but something fired in me, perhaps no more than the odd, inexplicable need we sometimes feel to open that book we'd long ago shoved into a corner of the closet, gaze at that one photograph again.

"All right," I said, giving no hint of what had actually determined my decision.

"Thanks, Roy. See you in a few minutes."

My father gave every intention of being entirely captured by an episode of *Petticoat Junction* when I walked into his room.

"I'm going out for a while," I told him.

His eyes stayed fixed on the screen.

"You need anything before I go?"

His gaze fell to his hands. His fingers uncurled, then curled again. "Listen here, Roy," he muttered. "I'd like for you to stay gone awhile. I just want to be by myself."

"All right, Dad. If you're sure you won't need me."

"Dead sure," he said.

Though it served as the county seat, Kingdom City was little more than a street along which shops and offices had been built, most of plain red brick. There was a barbershop complete with a twirling barber pole, the only sign in town that actually moved. The rest were made of tin or wood, with a smattering of pink or pale blue neon. Mr. Clark still had the drugstore I'd worked in as a boy, but Billings Hardware, where Archie had worked, sorting nails, stacking paint, mopping the floor, was now in other hands. I could still recall Mr. Billings's face in the days following Archie's arrest, how baffled he'd looked that the boy who'd worked for him, meekly obeyed a thousand petty orders, could explode so suddenly.

But it wasn't Archie I thought about that morning. It was Lila as I remembered her, a girl who'd seemed to take life as a dare.

You don't believe me, Roy? You don't believe I'll do it?

At first I'd thought her reckless, but it was really a fierce certainty that she could triumph over anything that drove her forward. I couldn't help but wonder what the woman would be like now.

Lonnie was outside his office when I arrived, propped back in a metal folding chair, a red Coca-Cola machine humming softly at his right. His cruiser stood freshly polished and gleaming a few feet away, the words "Sheriff Only" stenciled in bright yellow on the asphalt pavement beneath its rear bumper.

"I should be doing some paperwork, but it's just too damned hot inside," he said as I came toward him. "I been trying to get the county to buy me an air conditioner, but they won't do it." He tipped forward in his chair. "Thanks for coming in, Roy. I appreciate it. I really do."

"I doubt I can be of much help."

"I wouldn't be so sure of that," Lonnie said. He grinned. "Seemed to me like I caught a little spark there, buddy. A little spark still burning for you."

"I doubt it," I said. "Where is she?"

"First cell on your right."

"She's in the jail?"

Lonnie chuckled. "No, 'course not. I mean, she is, but the cell's not locked. Just a place for her to sit until she goes back home."

"So she can go home anytime she wants?"

"Well . . . no . . . not exactly. It's a protective-custody sort of thing. 'Cause she wouldn't say anything. About Spivey, I mean. She identified the body, but she wouldn't answer any questions about him. Not one. And no matter how you look at it, Clayton Spivey died under mysterious circumstances, which means that until Doc Poole takes a close look at the body, I got to assume there could have been foul play."

"What does any of this have to do with keeping Lila in a jail cell?"

"Like I told you, Roy, it's not locked. Of course, if you prefer, I could arrest her."

"For what?"

"Suspicious behavior."

"That's not a charge, and you know it."

"It'd stick long enough for me to find a better one if I needed to." He winked. "I'd just tell Judge Crowe I think it's pretty damn suspicious. This fellow found dead in the woods. A man that lived on her land."

"And only that," I said. "A tenant. With no other connection."

"Anyway, him dead in the woods and she won't have anything to do with me. A duly constituted authority. Hell, all I got to do is tell the judge she's not cooperating."

There was no point in arguing about it. Nothing had really changed in Kingdom County. Lonnie ran things in the same way his father had run them before him, with a cavalier certainty that he'd be protected by the old chain of command that flowed from the courthouse to the governor's mansion in one long, unbroken line of cronyism.

"Is Lila expecting me?" I asked.

"Nope," Lonnie answered. "You'll be a big surprise."

But from the expression on Lila's face, my sudden appearance was far more than a surprise. She looked astonished, as if she'd long ago dismissed me from her mind.

"Roy," she said quietly.

"Hello, Lila."

She sat on a metal cot covered by a thin striped mattress, her hands in her lap. Her hair had darkened but still threw off fiery tints. There were lines now at the corners of her eyes, and fainter ones crisscrossed her brow, but otherwise she appeared remarkably unchanged, no more than a blink away from the Highland beauty she'd been.

The cell door was open. I stepped inside.

"This is ridiculous," I told her. "Lonnie having you sit back here. Probably illegal too."

She gave a quick laugh. "He's trying to scare me. But it won't work." She smiled softly. "Lonnie told me you'd come back home," she said. Her gaze was steady, yet oddly probing. "He said you were a friend of his."

"I wouldn't go that far," I told her. "I just happened to be over at his house when we heard about Clayton Spivey."

She nodded. "I identified him this morning."

"I know," I told her. "And Lonnie should have let you go after that. There's no reason you should be —"

"He can't hold me, I know that," Lila said firmly. "Why are you here, Roy? Back in Kingdom County?"

"My father's dying," I answered. "I've come back to take care of him until it's over."

"Did you bring your family with you?"

"I don't have a family."

Shadows flitted behind her eyes. "I've thought of you a lot over the years."

I smiled. "We had some good times, didn't we?"

A vision formed in my mind. It was not just of myself and Lila, but of Archie too, and Gloria, all of us sitting at one of the little concrete picnic tables along the edge of the old rock quarry, Archie so moonstruck, so happy to be loved, he'd seemed almost to float in the warm spring air. Then it was only Archie I saw, sitting in his cell, reaching for my hand, *I ain't told the sheriff nothing, Roy, and I ain't going to.*

Her gaze darkened mysteriously, a storm cloud in her mind. "You knew what you wanted."

And what I'd wanted more than anything was Lila. Watching her now, I could see my own younger self in her eyes, the valley boy who'd spotted her at a dance, summoned the courage to approach her.

She drew in a long breath, and the dark cloud disappeared. "So, you finished college and stayed in California."

"A little town in the northern part of the state," I told her. "I teach at a school there."

"Good for you," Lila said. Her eyes lowered to her hands, then rose again. "Well, thanks for dropping by, Roy."

I knew that I was being dismissed, but I held my place at the entrance to the cell. "Lonnie tells me you're not saying much, Lila. About Clayton, I mean."

Her voice chilled. "I say as much as I want to say."

"Lonnie's just doing his job, you know. Just trying to find out a few things so that —"

"He's pretending he thinks Clayton Spivey was murdered," Lila interrupted sharply. "But I know better than that. Clayton had been sick for years. And lately he'd gotten a lot worse."

"Well, there was a gun near the body," I said, trying to put the best light on my detective-story understanding of Lonnie's tactics. "And so until Doc Poole can take a look, he has to assume that —"

"I came down to identify the body," Lila said, the fire of her youth suddenly returning. "I did it out of respect for Clayton. And it's all I'm going to do. I'm not at the beck and call of Lonnie Porterfield, and I never will be." She gazed at me in the way she had as a girl, eyes that peeled me back layer by layer. "I'm not going to play by Lonnie Porterfield's rules."

"I can see that."

"Good," she said. "Because I don't want to talk to Lonnie or about Lonnie."

With that, it was clear she'd closed the subject, and I half expected her to rise, stride out of the cell and through Lonnie's office, but she remained in place, her face brightening somewhat, as if hit by a ray of light.

"Remember that day at Taylor's Gorge?" she asked.

I saw her leap up from the blanket we'd spread across the ground.

You don't believe me, Roy? You don't believe I'll do it?

"Remember what we did?"

She was racing now, at full speed, toward the overhanging cliff, a gray wall that rose above the sparkling water.

"Yes, I remember."

I'd run after her, watching, amazed, as she hurtled forward, sleek as a deer over the forest floor, then out into the bright light that hung in a blinding curtain over the cliff's rocky ledge.

"Do you know what the best part was?" Lila asked.

She'd never slowed, never for an instant, but had dove out into the glittering air, her white feet like two small birds taking flight from the stony edge.

She stared at me now with the same willful gaze she'd had that afternoon. "The way you came running and leaped off that cliff right behind me."

I felt the earth fall away, its heavy pull release its grip, saw the dark water below.

She looked at me pointedly. "You wouldn't do that now, would you?"

"No."

She shrugged. "I guess I wouldn't either," she said.

Lonnie was sitting in his office when I left her a few minutes later. He plucked a thin cigar from his mouth, its white plastic tip well chewed. "Well, what'd she tell you?"

"Nothing. At least, nothing about Clayton."

"But she did talk to you, right?"

"Only about the old days. You know, when we were in high school together. I told her you needed to clear a few things up. That there was a gun near the body. She said she came down to identify the body, and that's all she's going to do."

Lonnie crushed the cigar against the sole of his shoe. "I just can't figure out why she won't answer a few questions and be done with it, Roy."

I knew the answer, saw Lila at my side, holding my hand, the two of us moving slowly down the road as the pickup closed upon us, then rattled past, a load of drunken boys slouched inside it, waving whiskey bottles in the dark air.

"I can't figure it out," Lonnie repeated.

"She doesn't have anything to hide," I told him.

He considered this a moment, then said, "Maybe you could help me out a little more on this, Roy." He nodded toward the overhanging hills. "Go back up to Waylord. Ask around. About Clayton. You know, among the neighbors. They'd talk to you, those people up there. You got roots up there."

"In Waylord? What roots? I've always lived in the valley."

"But your father's from up there. All they'd need to know is that you're Jesse Slater's son. They all remember him up there."

"Why would they remember my father?" I asked. "He left Waylord when he was sixteen. And as far as I know, he's never been back."

"Believe me, that won't matter," Lonnie insisted.

I shrugged. "I'm a schoolteacher, Lonnie, not a policeman. I don't know how to go about this sort of thing."

"It's just a little snooping around, that's all," Lonnie replied dismissively. "But I can make it official if you want me to." He pulled out the top drawer of his desk and plucked something from among a scattering of pads, pencils, and paper clips.

"Here you go," he said as he handed a badge to me.

I didn't take it. "I haven't agreed to this," I said.

"Look, Roy, you'd be doing a favor for Lila. Because if you go up there and ask a few questions, then I won't need to keep her down here with me anymore."

Lila's voice sounded in my ear, reminding me of the plunge I'd once been willing to take for her, along with her certainty that I would never do such a thing again.

I glanced at the badge. "You'd let her go now?"

"I sure would," Lonnie said. He smiled. "Now raise your right hand."

When I'd finished, he shook my hand. "Congratulations, Deputy Slater," he said with a laugh. "And welcome to the exciting world of law enforcement."

CHAPTER SEVEN

One thing was certain: I had no idea how to investigate anything. But I'd read a few detective stories over the years, and so I merely imitated what I thought a fictional sleuth would do, and went back to the place where Clayton Spivey's body had been found, in the hope that I might stumble upon something Lonnie had failed to notice.

The deeply shaded ground still bore the imprint of the body's dead weight, but nothing else. Lonnie had already collected whatever evidence he could find — the rifle, the shells, the rectangular cardboard box that had contained them.

Glancing here and there, I noticed nothing at all, until suddenly I glimpsed a second body.

It lay near the bank of the creek, and as I moved closer, I saw that it was a dove, its head shot off, the decaying body swarming with black ants.

Not far above, in a fork among the limbs, its nest rested, fully exposed, in dappled light.

The nest was empty now, but for a moment I imagined the dove curled inside its frail circle of twigs, peering down at Clayton Spivey, watching as he opened the ammunition box, drew out a single shell. I could see where one bullet had grazed the nest's supporting limb. Another had left a neat round hole in a gently swaying leaf. A third had actually penetrated the left side of the nest, through barely, merely grazing it enough to blow away a few twigs.

Through it all the dove had sat, strapped down by instinct, motionless, unable to take flight as is always the case with nesting doves, and waited for Spivey finally to steady his aim enough to put a bullet through its head.

"Afternoon, mister."

I turned and saw an old man a few feet away. He was clothed in overalls and a flannel shirt, both coated with the region's red dust. He'd tugged his hat from his head before speaking to me, and now held it with both hands, a gesture common to the people of Waylord.

"Name's Crenshaw," the man said. "Nate Crenshaw. I live up the creek a ways."

He was not threatening in any way and yet a threat seemed to rest between us like a pistol on a gaming table.

"You the law?" he asked.

It struck me with some relief that in fact I was. I took out the badge. "Roy Slater." I nodded toward where the body had lain. "It was Clayton Spivey we found here. I guess you heard about that."

Crenshaw continued to watch me warily. "Yeah, I heard about it."

"Did you know him?"

The old man shook his head. "Not much, no. He sure run into a patch of bad luck, didn't he?"

Bad luck.

It was the same phrase my father had always used to gather into one pile a vast array of disasters. Children drowned because of bad luck. Babies died of whooping cough and meningitis for the same reason. When men went to prison or were crushed in collapsing mines, bad luck was the culprit. Women dead in childbirth, or ground down by labor. Bad luck. Once, when I'd asked my father why he'd left Waylord, he'd simply shrugged and said, "Too much bad luck up there."

"I seen Clayton sometimes," Crenshaw added. "Not too often though. He wasn't too sociable. Lived out in the woods. By hisself."

"How'd he make a living?"

Crenshaw shrugged. "He swapped things. He wasn't in good enough shape to work regular."

"Did he have any friends?"

"He visited Lila Cutler from time to time. She let him stay in that little shack on her land. Felt sorry for him, I guess."

"Was that their only connection?" I asked.

"That he lived on her property?"

Crenshaw nodded. "Far as I know. Never heard Lila say there was anything else to it. 'Course, Lila's quiet."

But the girl I remembered sang along with the band when we danced, hummed continually, called loudly to me from her seat in a darkened theater or the crowded assembly hall at school or one of the wooden bleachers that lined the football field, her arm in the air, waving energetically. *Over here, Roy.*

"She was lively when I knew her," I said. "In high school."

"Maybe so," Crenshaw said. He eyed the stream briefly, turning something over in his mind. "Clayton was out hunting, I guess," he said, nodding toward the dove's body.

"I suppose he was."

Crenshaw walked to the edge of the creek, picked up a stick, and dipped it gently into the water. "Hunting like a feller that's hungry."

He drew the stick from the water, considered its wet tip, then lowered it back into the stream, moving its tip in ever-tightening circles over the surface of the water.

"Like a feller that ain't got time to wait for a deer or a rabbit. Because he's hungry. Needs whatever he can get."

"Was Clayton Spivey that poor?" I asked.

Crenshaw tossed the stick into the creek. "Must have been, or he wouldn't have been shooting at no dove." His eyes drifted up toward the shattered nest. "A dove won't fly, you know. Just sets there till you shoot it." He continued to peer at the nest, looking more and more puzzled as the seconds passed. Finally he shook his head slowly, as if giving in to the mystery of things. "Maybe that's why Clayton was after it. 'Cause he was too weak to go after nothing else."

I looked at the dove, her bloodied feathers alive with ants. "Lila told me that he was sick. Was he dying?"

"Heard he was, yes, sir."

"What of?"

"Black lung."

Then I knew exactly what had happened to Clayton Spivey, the sudden seizure that had overtaken him, driving him first to his knees, then forward, pressing his face against the ground, blood rising like a geyser in his throat.

"Ain't no cure once you got it," Crenshaw added.

No cure, and nothing to do but wait until the moment comes for you to drown in your own blood.

And, I thought, case closed.

I was almost halfway down the mountain when I saw another house sweep into view, one Lila had taken me to many years before and which I associated with her so powerfully, she seemed almost to appear in my car as I neared the building once again, a red-haired girl sitting at my side as she had that day. "Pull in there, Roy," she'd said, pointing to a rutted driveway, "I want you to meet my second mother."

Her name was Juanita Her-Many-Horses, and I'd thought her ancient, though she'd certainly been no more than forty-five at that time, her skin still smooth and brown, with deep-set eyes that shone darkly, like her hair, her features as Indian as her last name.

"You're a good-looking boy," she'd said when I came to a halt before her. "You and Lila going steady now?"

"Yes, ma'am, we are."

More than twenty years had passed since that day, and I suppose I could easily have continued on past the old house. I'd done it only the day before, when Lonnie and I had made our way up to Lila's home. But now the past was a rope stretched out to me, tugging me back toward those long-forgotten days.

"Don't want no Bibles," she called as I got out of my car. "Got all the Bibles I need already."

"I'm not selling Bibles," I called back.

"Don't want no medicines neither."

"I'm not selling anything," I assured her, then made my way toward where she sat beneath the shade of a large elm, cooling herself with a paper fan that bore a figure of

Jesus in flowing robes.

She dug in her lap for a pair of glasses. "You come from down around, I bet."

Down around. The name she'd always given to the valley that lay below her.

"You don't remember me, Juanita? I'm Roy Slater."

Her eyes flashed in recognition. "You the one from down around. Went with Lila way back when."

"Yes."

She smiled widely, revealing gaps in her teeth. "You come plenty of times that summer."

A bright hot summer, the cool streams our only relief, Lila in her cutoff jeans and a white blouse knotted at the waist. I'd come so often, Lila such a fire in my mind, that Archie had teased me about it. *Speeding the way you do, that girl will be the death of you, Roy.* By then he'd been hardly less smitten than I was, his passionate attention so firmly settled upon Gloria Kellogg, he'd seemed unable to think of anything else.

Juanita Her-Many-Horses nodded thoughtfully. "You the one that went off to school. And never come back for Lila."

"She told me not to," I said softly.

Juanita glanced over to where a pigsty rested in a dense cloud of stink a hundred yards away. Near its center, an enormous sow lay in the steamy mud, swarms of greenflies rising each time it shifted or twitched its flanks, then descending again, to feed on the muck that surrounded it.

"Call him Amos and Andy," Juanita said with a laugh when she noticed me looking at the pig. " 'Cause he done already big enough for two. Call him Amos for short."

I nodded toward a stack of cinder blocks opposite her. "Mind if I sit with you a few minutes?"

"Don't mind, no," Juanita said. "You seen Lila since you been back?"

"Yes, I have."

"Seen her go down the road this morning."

"She went to Kingdom City. She should be back soon."

"How come she went down there?"

"To identify a body," I answered. "Clayton Spivey. He died over on Jessup Creek. They found him in the woods yesterday."

Juanita considered this for a moment. "Guess they'll be burying him right soon. Can't go to the funeral though. Ain't got the energy for it. You come to help Lila some way?"

"No, I was just on my way back down the mountain. I came up to check a few things out. For the sheriff."

Juanita grimaced. "Don't like that sheriff."

"No one up here does," I said.

" 'Cause of his daddy," Juanita said. "The old sheriff. 'Cause of the way he done people way back when. Always going up and down the road in that big car of his."

I turned toward the road and saw Wallace Porterfield as I thought Juanita Her-Many-Horses must have seen him years before, huge and weighty behind the wheel of his cruiser, prowling the roads of Waylord like a ravenous wolf. "Always looking for bad things on people. You must of heard that."

"Why would I have heard it?"

" 'Cause he was looking for dirt on Lila's mama."

"When was this?"

"That summer you was coming up to see Lila. Done it all summer. All fall. Didn't stop till winter. Guess he figured he couldn't find nothing on her, so he just give up." She looked at me shrewdly. "Or maybe he just figured she already had trouble enough. What with Lila going through all that trouble, you know, because of your brother. Them killings."

The dark hedge that bordered County Road surfaced in my mind, the lights from my car cruising down it until they reached Archie's old Ford.

"Anyway, the sheriff never asked me about Betty after that. Just let her be, didn't come asking no more."

"He never came again after the murders?"

"Not to me, he didn't," Juanita said. "Guess he got what he was after. Or figured he never would."

CHAPTER EIGHT

It was only midday when I reached the out-
skirts of Kingdom City, my mind now focused on the abruptly foreshortened lives that
my conversation with Juanita Her-Many-
Horses had conjured up again. Archie's, of
course, but also the two people who'd been
murdered on that catastrophic night, a man
and woman who'd seemed old to me then,
already halfway to the grave despite the fact
that at the time of their deaths Horace and
Lavenia Kellogg had been scarcely older than
I was now.

I knew that Mrs. Kellogg had had no time
to consider her death as the bullet pierced
the back of her skull. Only her husband, shot
repeatedly, might have glimpsed the years
that were being blasted from him as the bullets struck his arm, his leg, the small of his
back.

There were hours to kill before sunset, and
I had no idea how to kill them. I might stroll
through town, of course, chat with the few
people who still recognized me from the old
days. But those chance meetings had always
left me with a lingering unease. Even in the
warmest smiles, or couched within the most

casual exchanges, I saw and heard a question that went unasked, the one about Archie: *Why did he do it, Roy?*

And so I didn't go back to Kingdom City that afternoon. Instead, I revisited the old fishing spots and swimming holes to which Archie and I had so often gone.

At Calvin Pond I remembered Archie in his blond innocence, able to pluck dragonflies from the air as if they floated on it languidly, like feathers. He would hold them by the wings, turn them slowly, studying the shifting iridescent colors of their bodies in the sunlight, *See how they go rainbow.*

On Fulton Creek, I recalled him with a cane pole, a cork bobbing in the water. He'd always claimed that a "big one" lurked along the shadowy embankment, named the trout Cecil, and sworn that one day he'd yank it from the water, then hunker down and eat it raw, "like bobcats do."

Late in the afternoon, I stood alone on Saddle Rock, the huge granite slab where Archie and I had made camp on the night we'd finally run away. By sundown we'd gotten no more than five miles from home. As darkness fell, we climbed onto the rock, then plopped down on the single blanket we called our "bedroll," and prepared to wait out the night.

Our father had found us two hours later. He'd spotted Scooter on the road, the faithful dog who'd followed us from home. We'd not thought to keep Scooter at our side for the night, and so he'd wandered down the rock and was sitting quietly at its base when our father's truck came rattling up the road. The old man had stormed up the side of the rock seconds later, Scooter loping happily at his side. He'd jerked us from our sleep and driven us like sheep back to his car, shoving us all the way, muttering curses at our backs, most of them aimed at me, since he'd known quite clearly that I was the one who'd plotted the escape, then dragged Archie, innocent and foolish, into my scheme, *Ten years old, where the hell you think you was going, Roy? And with Archie, who ain't got sense enough to say no to you.*

At home he'd sent us, hungry and tired, to our room, where we'd spent the night speculating on the punishment that was sure to come, the long days of mockery that were in store for us, my father's disdain poured like an acid over our heads, and compared to which we would have preferred fifty lashes from his belt.

But as I stood at the place where Archie and I had huddled together so long ago, I didn't dwell on any of that. Instead, I recalled the shooting star we'd seen that night, Archie's eyes filled with childlike awe, tracing its long fall across the nightbound sky.

He would not look so lost in wonder again

until Gloria appeared many years later, offering Archie a love that looked past his awkwardness, his shyness, the slow movement of his mind, the fact that he had nothing to offer in return but his own guileless heart. I could still recall his determination to keep her. *I'll do anything, Roy. Anything.*

We'd been standing in the darkness outside our house when he said that, a frigid wind in the pine, Lila a few yards away, wrapped in a thick wool coat, her red hair flowing over her shoulders as she leaned against my old Chevy. She'd had only one question when I came back to the car.

Roy, what's he going to do?

My answer, once given, had never changed.

I don't know.
But he's so . . . ?
Get in the car, Lila.
You can't just leave him like this, Roy.
Get in the car.
But . . .
Let's go.

The school we'd attended as boys was a small redbrick building, a WPA project from start to finish, solid but uninspired. To Archie it had been a prison, a place he hated and in which he was often humiliated. But school provided sweet relief to me, a refuge where I'd sit alone in the library, lose myself in a book, the lone "intellectual," as I sometimes thought of myself, among boys who regarded school as entirely corrosive, reading an activity that turned them into sissies while sports turned them into men.

I'd left the playing fields to Archie, hoping that he might do on the ball field what he couldn't do in the classroom, watching him try his best, give it his all, in game after game. For most of those years I watched alone, but during that final year Gloria sometimes sat beside me, clapping wildly at Archie's smallest achievements, a base hit or a fly to center field that he actually managed to catch.

A group of children was playing in that same field behind the school that night, and since my only other option was to return to the steamy atmosphere of my father's house, I decided to watch the game for a while.

The bleachers were only half filled with spectators, most of them young parents eager to watch their kids take a turn at bat. The children on the field were dressed in crisp white uniforms and dark blue caps, far different from the boys who'd played years before. We'd had no uniforms in those days, no elaborate equipment.

Watching the parents cheer and clap, I remembered that my father had rarely come to watch Archie play. Exhausted from working on a road crew or hauling pulpwood, he'd usually flopped onto the sofa, then fallen into a fitful, muttering sleep.

And yet there were times when he'd actually tried to fulfill some part of his fatherhood. He'd taught us both to drive, though impatiently, barking harshly each time we swerved into the dirt siding. He'd tried to teach us to fly-fish as well, grumbling at how poorly we did it but persisting in the effort until our incompetence finally overwhelmed him and he gave up, yanking the poles from our hands and stomping off toward the car.

And sometimes he would suddenly show up at a night game to watch Archie play, though his eyes seemed only distantly to follow the flight of the ball or a boy's frantic run around the bases. But unlike the other fathers, he never leapt to his feet when Archie did something right. He seemed simply to appear at random, watch the game in silence, leave without speaking either to Archie or to me.

I'd thought then that it had been an effort, however halting, to play the father. But looking back now, remembering the few times my father had come to watch Archie play, I realized that his attendance had not actually been random at all, that he'd come only to particular games, the ones in which Archie's team had been arrayed against the team from Waylord.

The Waylord team.

A scruffy crew of impoverished boys, the sons of miners and raw subsistence farmers, the riffraff of the hills, dressed in hand-me-downs, with dirty caps and ripped shirts, teeth blackened by poor care, poor diet, some whose skin even bore the glossy patina of malnutrition. They were a spirited group nonetheless, and it was said by valley boys that in the Waylord fields the bases were made of feed sacks filled with sand, and that the boys themselves played without gloves, and sometimes with hard round stones rather than balls, stones they batted into the air at terrific speed, using long lead pipes. Compared to them, the Kingdom City boys felt themselves curiously soft and pampered, blessed never to have known all that made the boys of Waylord hard and tough and filled with an oddly haunting pride, theirs a poverty so deep, it made our spare circumstances appear luxurious in comparison, and filled our hearts with awe.

That evening, as I sat in the same bleachers where my father had sometimes lingered in sullen silence, eyes fixed on the lighted field, I tried to imagine why he had come to see the Waylord team, tried to think through the baffling loyalty he'd shown toward the very people he'd seemed in all other ways to despise, often mouthing horrendous oaths against them, how hopeless they were, how weak and stupid, how much by their own hands they did damage to themselves.

What call had occasionally roused him from the orange sofa, despite his weariness after a long workday and sent him down to the playing field in the sweltering summer darkness, to sit in the hazy light, apart from the other parents, as if refusing to be drawn into life's domestic circle?

I knew that it was not a question I would ever ask him, nor one he would answer even if I did. When he died, any hope that I might ever learn how he'd come to be the man he was would die too. And yet the fact that time was running out on these mysteries bothered me very little. Long ago I had come to accept that they were beyond solution, my father a closed door where the sign had always been posted, *Keep Out.*

CHAPTER NINE

He was sitting on the front porch when I got to the house later that night, leaning back in a rickety chair, his bony feet propped up on an overturned tin bucket. He nodded coolly as I got out of the car but waited until I reached the porch to speak.

"Why don't you go on back to California, Roy. I been thinking about it all day, and the way I see it, there's just no need for you to hang around here. I'm doing fine."

Until earlier that afternoon I might have taken my father up on his offer, packed my things and driven home. But now I saw Lila in the jail cell, still like no one else I'd ever met, with nothing at all diminished from the girl I'd once loved. I felt compelled to see her through the current trouble, at least as far as keeping an eye on Lonnie Porterfield was concerned. I needed to make sure he did not renege on the promise he'd made me to leave her alone.

"No, I'm going to hang around for a while, Dad," I told him. "Does it bother you that much, having me around?"

"Suit yourself," he said absently, then added, "Hey, you didn't happen to buy some cigarettes while you was out, did you?"

I sat down on the top step. "I'll get you some in the morning."

"In the morning, right."

His tone instantly rankled me with its suggestion that I knew nothing of what a man needed to make it through the night.

"I'm not going back into town tonight, if that's what you're getting at," I told him. "Not for cigarettes or anything else."

"Who asked you to, Roy? I can do without 'em. Besides, if I wanted cigarettes, I'd get 'em myself."

"I wouldn't advise it."

Now it was my father's turn to bristle. " 'I wouldn't advise it,' " he repeated prissily. "That all you learned in college, Roy? To talk that way. Like old Miss Danforth, that damn old bitch I had. 'A *kid* is a *goat*,' she used to say. 'It *ain't* children.' Always strutting around. With her nose in the air like us kids stunk up the schoolhouse. 'Can't' means 'ain't able to,' she used to say, 'may' means 'could I do it if you let me.' Damn old bitch. Thought she was better than us. Come up from Kingdom City to teach us poor, hopeless little bastards how to talk right. You remind me of her."

I started to reply, but he waved me into silence.

"But hell, it wouldn't have mattered how that damn old bitch talked to me. I wouldn't have stayed in school nohow. Didn't have no use for it. Couldn't see how it would do me no good."

To break the silence that fell between us, I told him, "I stopped by the old ball field this evening. Holbrook was playing Kingdom City."

"Be a wonder if either one of them got a single run. Squirts, far as I can see in the paper."

"When was the last time you went to a game?"

He leaned forward and spat into the yard. "Years."

"You came a few times back when I was a kid," I reminded him. "To see Archie play."

"Archie wasn't bad," my father said. "Hit fairly good." A tiny smile flickered. "You 'member that night he hit that homer against Waylord?"

I was surprised that my father remembered it, although I recalled vividly how the ball had sailed upward and upward, made its high, graceful arc over center field, brought the crowd roaring to its feet as my brother rounded the bases.

"Yeah, I do."

I'd glanced up into the bleachers as Archie loped toward second base, expecting to see my father where he'd been sitting minutes before, perhaps even thinking that he might be on his feet like everyone else, cheering madly, clapping his hands.

But the spot where he'd sat was vacant.

"That was a good night for Archie, I guess," my father said in a tone that was unusual for him, almost wistful.

My eyes had scanned the bleachers, desperate to find my father, to reassure myself that he'd seen the ball rise, was at that instant watching as Archie rounded the bases slowly, gracefully, soaking up the crowd's wild praise.

"Never hit another one, Archie didn't," my father added now. "Never hit another homer his whole damn life."

I'd looked back toward the field in time to see Archie touch third base, by then merely prancing along, his own eyes searching the bleachers for the spot where he'd seen our father moments before, empty now, hollow, my brother's triumphant smile fading slowly, until, at home plate, it had vanished altogether.

My father casually scratched the gray stubble on the side of his face. "Just lost interest in playing ball, I guess. Archie did."

It was only then, after Archie had scored, that I'd caught sight again of my father. He'd left the bleachers and was now standing beside a woman, full-figured in a satiny blue dress, blond hair bobbed, glancing over her shoulder to reveal glistening red lips, a blush at her cheek, the younger version of an older face I'd not seen again until years later, after I'd found my way up to Waylord, where she had greeted me at the door, *Well, now, you must be Roy Slater. Lila's not quite ready.*

"Betty Cutler was at that game," I said.

"That right?" My father seemed hardly to recognize the name.

"You don't remember talking to her?"

"Why would I remember that?"

"Last night you mentioned that you knew each other. Betty-and-Deidre, remember?"

"I knew a lot of people up in Waylord way back when."

"I just thought that —"

"Talked to a lot of people at them games too."

"Well, actually, you didn't," I said. "You sat off by yourself. I don't remember ever seeing you talk to anybody but —"

"What difference does it make who I talked to at them games?"

"It's just an observation, Dad."

A brief silence, then he said, "You see Lila today?"

"Yes."

"What'd she have to say?"

"Nothing much."

He shrugged. "If you don't want to talk about it, just say so."

"We talked about the old days," I said. "High school. She didn't have much to say."

But my father no longer seemed interested

in my conversation with Lila. His mind was now focused on a gloomier terrain. "Death clams people up. Did that to your mother."

He was talking about Archie, of course, the way his death had sent my mother into the murky bedroom for the rest of her days. But I wondered if he were not also talking about others who'd suffered the same devastation, the process by which a child's death closes around a parent's world, becomes the dark prism through which all life passes after that.

"Lonnie Porterfield should just leave Lila alone." His eyes snapped over to me. "If Lila don't want to talk, it ain't none of his business to make her."

"He asked me to help him." I drew out the badge Lonnie had issued me. "He even made it official."

As if I'd pulled a rattlesnake from my pocket, my father recoiled physically. "You ain't got no business carrying that thing."

"Why not? Lonnie made me a deputy."

Even as I spoke, it seemed perverse to me that in some boyish way I still wanted to impress my father.

"A sheriff's deputy ain't nothing but a gun-thug with a badge." The mining wars flared in his eyes. "Bought and sold by the mine owners."

"County deputies don't work for mine owners anymore," I said, now sorry that I'd bothered to display the badge.

"What do you know about what deputies do or don't do around here, Roy?"

"I know that things have changed, Dad."

"Things don't never change. People neither. Especially them Porterfields. You take off the muzzle, and Lonnie'll come at you just like his old man come at me."

"What did Wallace Porterfield ever do to you?"

My father waved his hand. "You don't know a thing, Roy. All that learning, them books you read, and you still don't know one goddamn thing."

I glanced at his hands and couldn't help but admire how steady they remained.

"Tell me something then," I challenged. "Tell me something I don't know."

His eyes blazed. "All right, I will. Here's something you don't know. Blood is blood. What's in the blood is there for good. You can't get shed of it."

I stared at him silently.

"Well?" he asked after a moment.

"That's it? That's the thing I don't know?"

"Damn right it is. 'Cause if you knew it, you wouldn't be carrying no badge Lonnie Porterfield give you." He snorted harshly. "But you're going to learn a lesson soon enough, by God." His voice rang with a maddening certainty that made all further argument superfluous. "The fact is, Lonnie's just using you, Roy. Getting you to do something

108

'cause he don't want to do it hisself. Just like his daddy used people. Give them little tin badges and got them to go against their own kind. They come up like they owned Waylord and everybody in it. Come up in them big cars from Kingdom City. In them fine clothes they wore. Like they could beat us at anything. Whip us and make us give in to 'em."

His eyes were like flares in the darkness, and in that instant I knew why he'd come to the playing field at night all those many years ago, why he'd come only when the boys of Waylord played the boys of Kingdom City, the hills against the valley. He had come to see them beat us, beat to a pulp the Kingdom City team, shame and humiliate it, trample it beneath their bare callused feet. He had despised the sons of the valley that much . . . or that much loved the sons of those he'd left behind.

"Hell, I figure the only reason Lonnie wants you around is 'cause he thinks it's exciting," he said offhandedly.

"Why would Lonnie find having me around exciting, Dad?"

"Why do you have to keep at things, Roy? Bite and scratch. Bite and scratch. Just like that old mangy dog."

That old dog. Scooter.

Then I knew.

"Because of Archie," I said. "You think

Lonnie finds it exciting to have me around because of the murders?"

I waited for him to answer, feeling strangely accused while I waited, but he only leaned forward abruptly, drew a crumpled pack of cigarettes from his shirt pocket, thumped one out, and grabbed it with his teeth.

"I thought you were out of cigarettes," I said.

"I never said I was out." He plucked a match from the same pocket and raked it across the bottom of his shoe. "Will be by morning though."

He brought the match to the cigarette, and in the light that washed up from it, I noticed the first hint of yellow in the whites of his eyes, a sign, according to Doc Poole, that his liver had begun to fail.

"Glad I didn't go with you," he said, his face now clothed in darkness once again. "That last night. Glad I didn't go see him that last time."

He was talking about Archie again.

"Didn't want to go with you that night. Didn't see no reason to after the way he got to sputtering the time I seen him. Figured maybe I caused it. All that sputtering. Didn't want him to get all upset like that again." He shifted uncomfortably in his seat. "So I didn't go."

"No, you didn't," I said quietly.

" 'Cause of the way he acted the time I visited him," my father said, now returning to the one and only time he'd visited Archie in jail. "Didn't want to see that again."

It had been a cold, rainy night in January, muddy roads until we reached the main highway, my mother in her Sunday clothes, a black dress with a little pillbox hat, her face covered with black netting, clutching a tattered Bible. Archie had been arrested at just after dawn that same morning, and was now to spend his first night in the county jail. Even so, my father had resisted the idea of visiting him — *Don't want to see him behind bars* — but had finally agreed to accompany us to Kingdom City, where he'd balked again, refusing to go into the sheriff's office, relenting in his refusal only after my mother had made a tearful plea.

"Wished I'd stayed at home." He tossed the match out into the yard. "Didn't want to see Archie like that. Crying and sputtering."

"It was his first night in jail."

"Whining like he done. Telling Wallace Porterfield how sorry he was. Messing his pants."

"Messing his pants? What are you talking about, Dad? Archie didn't mess his pants."

"Figured he did. Before. When Porterfield went at him. Wanting to know what happened. Threatening him. Scaring him."

"What makes you think Sheriff Porterfield

did anything like that?"

"The old lady never said a word," my father blurted out, his mind now whipsawing away from Archie. "Never one word about what Archie done to hisself after ya'll left him there that last time."

Instead, she'd taken to her bed, where she remained, balled up beneath the quilt, hour after hour, day after day, sinking ever deeper into the religious mania that would consume her mind during the few weeks that remained to her.

"Just went right to bed after she found out about it," my father said. "Didn't say one damn word. Just went to the bedroom."

Did I have any clear memory of my mother ever coming out of that room again? Ever joining my father and me at the table? No, never at her sewing again, or her crocheting, gone within a few weeks, gone forever, gone to Jesus.

"She couldn't take Archie's death," I said.

I glanced over to where my father sat in stony silence, lost in thought, until he finally said, "Never could figure out why he done it. Hung hisself like that. With nothing but a bedsheet to do it with. Wanting to die that bad. Wanting to get out of it. Not giving nobody no reason for it. Couldn't see Archie doing that."

"Well, he did," I said firmly, trying to get past such fruitless speculation, the image it called up in my brain, Archie hanging from the top of his bunk, eyes popped, tongue black and swollen.

"The old lady always mothered him," my father said. "You too. Always mothering Archie. Day and night. Telling him what to do."

"We had to, Dad. Archie needed —"

"Archie needed to be a man. To die like a man. Not apologizing to everybody, whining about how sorry he was, how he didn't mean it, how it was something just come over him. A miserable thing, sniveling like a baby, apologizing to the whole goddamn world." He drew in a long, smoldering breath. "Porterfield standing there, grinning the whole time."

"Archie just wanted people to understand that he hadn't meant to do it," I said. "That he'd just . . . that it was . . . a mistake."

My father peered out into the blackness. "All for Horace Kellogg's daughter."

Horace Kellogg's daughter.

It was the only name my father had ever called Gloria.

She'd lived in a big house a mile or so from town, the oldest child of Horace and Lavenia Kellogg, merchant pillars of our community, a slight, willowy girl with dark blue eyes and pale white skin. At times she'd seemed fixed in a dark anticipation, a mood Archie had worked to lift, bringing his face

113

very near hers, staring eye to eye, cocking his head playfully, grinning, *Come out of it now, Gloria. Don't stay holed up in there.*

"He loved Gloria," I said.

"Then he should have took her and been done with it."

"He tried, didn't he?"

"Yes, he did," my father said, suddenly growing curiously meditative. "He did try." He plucked the cigarette from his mouth and threw it onto the ground. "Surprised me that he did. I mean, all by hisself like that."

I heard my brother's voice. *Will you go with me, Roy?*

My father stared out into the darkness. "It was Horace Kellogg that caused it. Putting that daughter of his through all kinds of hell. Telling her she was just trash for running around with such as Archie. Archie knew what Kellogg was like. That's why he took that gun. 'Cause he knowed that bastard wouldn't never have set there and let his girl go off with the likes of Archie."

"How would Archie have known that? I don't think he ever so much as spoke to Horace Kellogg."

"Everybody knows what Horace Kellogg is like, Roy. Horace Kellogg and Wallace Porterfield. They're one and the same."

"In what way?"

"In that they ain't got no use for a boy like Archie. You think for one minute Horace

Kellogg would have stood by and let Archie marry that puny little daughter of his? No, sir, he wouldn't have put up with that. But I still wouldn't have told Archie to let her go, like you done Lila Cutler."

My father seemed to realize that he'd reached some kind of line in me and dropped the subject.

"Well, I think I'll turn in." He struggled to his feet with a groan. "Good night, Roy."

"Good night," I said crisply, then watched as he headed for the door, moving toward it unsteadily, like a leaking boat.

Every instinct demanded that I let him go, and yet a small question nagged at me, the sort that, if left unanswered, pursues us through the years, becomes a ghostly whisper, a rumor carried by the rain, about something we don't know and yet suspect must have in secrecy and stealth deranged and finally undone our lives.

And so I said, "You think I told Archie to let Gloria go? When would I have done that, Dad?"

"That night."

"What makes you think I saw Archie that night?"

" 'Cause Porterfield come asking. The next morning. When he come to tell the old lady about the killings and how he had Archie in jail over in Kingdom City."

"Where was I when he came here?"

"You'd already gone to work, like me," my father answered. "At the drugstore."

I recalled that morning, Saturday, the night's snow long melted away by a warm morning sun, leaving the streets of Kingdom City slick and gleaming.

"What did the sheriff want to know?" I asked.

"Where you'd been," my father answered. "When Archie done it. She told him you was probably up in Waylord. That you'd been out with Lila that night."

In my mind I saw Porterfield stride past the window of Clark's Drugs as he had that morning, his eyes leveled upon me as I stood, wiping glasses, behind the soda fountain.

"Porterfield saw me that morning," I said. "In the drugstore. But he didn't come in. He never asked me anything about where I was that night."

I remembered how, two days later, when Porterfield had led me silently down the corridor to Archie's cell for what turned out to be our last time together, he had wheeled and walked back to his office without so much as a word, the sound of dangling keys the only ones I'd heard.

"And when I went to visit Archie, he never asked me one question about the murders."

My father nodded. "Archie wasn't a bad boy. Just too much like me, that's all. Had the same bad luck."

CHAPTER TEN

As I made his morning coffee, I knew he was awake just beyond his bedroom door, waiting for me to leave so he could enjoy the only thing he seemed really capable of enjoying, his granite solitude.

I tapped at the closed door, waited, then called, "Your coffee's ready." When no answer came, I placed his brown mug on the kitchen table. "It'll be cold in five minutes," I added.

With that I considered my morning obligations done and headed into town, driven by some priggish sense of duty to report to Lonnie.

Lonnie didn't appear at all surprised to see me. "Well, I let Lila go like I said I would," he told me with a friendly wink. "You two hook up later?"

He saw the expression on my face and laughed a crudely insinuating laugh that reminded me of the sliminess that had always been a part of his character. "You didn't?" he said. "I figured you'd have cashed in by now. You know, got a little something for that favor you did her."

I heard my father's warning, *Blood is blood.*

Them Porterfields just use people, and considered the dark world they suggested, all of us bound to the stake of our birthright, anchored in the deep sludge of the generations, not at all born into a wide, bright world, but carelessly tossed into the web.

"The fact is, it wasn't doing any good to keep her here anyway," Lonnie added now. "I released Clayton's body too. No reason to keep it."

"Well, I found out that Clayton Spivey was —"

"Dying?" Lonnie interrupted with a triumphant grin.

"Yes."

"I found out before you did, I bet," he said. "Doc Poole finished the autopsy just after you left."

He looked surprised when I picked up the report from his desk.

"Natural causes, according to Doc Poole," he said. "Old Clayton just spit blood and died."

"Byssinosis," I said, then continued to scan the report, noting the basic facts Doc Poole had recorded in it. He'd written "none" in the space provided for next of kin.

"So that's it, Roy," Lonnie said when I handed him back the report. "Case closed."

"Have you told Lila?" I asked.

Lonnie shook his head. "Nope."

"Mind if I do it?"

A grin slithered onto his lips. "Why, you old dog, you," he said, an answer I took to be yes.

I turned toward the door, but Lonnie called me back. "That badge," he said. "I better get that back from you now."

I plucked the badge from my pocket and placed it on Lonnie's desk.

"Remember now, Roy, you're not going to be acting in an official capacity anymore," Lonnie said with a leering wink. "I mean, in whatever you have in mind for your old girl-friend up in Waylord."

"What would I have in mind, Lonnie?"

A broad smile crossed Lonnie's face. "Maybe offering a little comfort," he said. "Nothing wrong in that."

I pulled into Lila's driveway a few minutes later.

At the top of the stairs, I hesitated outside the door, feeling intensely foolish now, a middle-aged man mired in a high-school romance. So foolish in fact that I might have turned and fled had Lila not come upon me suddenly.

"Roy." She stood at the corner of the house, a basket of vegetables in her hand. "I just came from the garden. "Mama's sleeping." She nodded toward the house. "She's not really able to take care of herself anymore."

"Doc Poole gave Lonnie his report," I told

her. "Clayton Spivey died of black lung. The case is closed as far as Lonnie's concerned."

She straightened herself abruptly. "I don't care what Lonnie Porterfield does. I'm trash to him. Always have been."

It had been a hot summer night, Lila and I walking beside the road together, holding hands, a pickup truck roaring past, a load of valley boys in the back, waving bottles, yelling drunkenly, Lonnie in the midst of them, louder than the rest, taunting as he went by, *Be careful, Roy, Waylord girls ain't never fresh.*

"He was drunk," I told her, repeating the same excuse for Lonnie I'd offered my father only a day before. "He was young."

"Yes, he was," Lila replied. "Anyway, I knew what he thought about me after that. The same way his father felt. That the girls up here are just something to be used. Something to be played with."

"You sound like my father. The way he hates the Porterfields."

"Maybe I am like your father, Roy."

"You're not in the least like him."

She smiled. "You didn't look at me like other boys."

"I was shy," I said.

She grew still beneath my gaze.

"I would have come back, you know. After college. I would have come back for you if you hadn't . . ."

"None of that matters now," Lila said.

It was then I suddenly glimpsed Lila's life as I thought she had come to see it, as something that had flowed grimly out of our teenage romance, a stream that should have been bright and glittering but had grown dark and murky.

"Lila . . . I . . ."

A voice from inside the house called her name.

"My mother," Lila said hastily. "I've got to go."

I reached for her arm. "Lila . . ."

Our eyes locked for an instant, then the screen door creaked open and a thin, raw-boned woman emerged from the darkened house, a mere shadow of the woman I'd first glimpsed in a metallic blue dress in the bleachers.

"Who's that?" she called.

"We have company," Lila told her. "A gentleman caller, you might say." She moved past me, her eyes fixed on her mother. "Do you remember him, Mama?"

Betty Cutler leaned forward, now squinting so hard, her eyes were mere slits. The name that broke from her lips chilled me to the bone.

"Jesse," she whispered.

"No, Mama." Lila took her mother's arm. "This is Roy. Roy Slater. Not Jesse."

The old woman drew away from me instantly.

"He's just come up to visit." Lila tugged her mother back toward the door. "Isn't that nice?"

The old woman's hand fell limply to her side. Something in her eyes grew dark and accusatory. "You ain't the man your daddy was."

"Mama!" Lila blurted out. "You be quiet now."

The old woman's voice hardened. "Jesse wouldn't have took it."

"Mama, stop it," Lila said sharply.

But Mrs. Cutler didn't stop. "Jesse would have done something about it."

"Let's go back in the house, Mama," Lila pleaded.

Mrs. Cutler's eyes remained level upon mine. "Even after what they done to him at the Waylord mine."

I stared at her helplessly. "The Waylord mine?"

"Come on now, Mama," Lila snapped, firmly turning the old woman away from me, whispering, "Sorry, Roy, sorry," as she ushered her toward the door.

I waited in the yard, all but reeling from so disturbing a remark, the sound of it echoing through my brain. Through the window I could see Lila guide her mother hastily toward a wooden rocker, scolding her gently all the way.

In response, the old woman muttered

something I couldn't understand.

"Mama just says things, Roy," Lila told me when she returned to me.

"What was she talking about?" I pressed.

"I don't know," Lila said. "She gets things confused. One memory floats into another one. Things whirl around."

She knew that I'd seen it, the lie in her eyes. "I better get back inside," she said quietly. "Good-bye, Roy."

She backed away from me, her smile soft, almost fragrant, like a small pale flower on her lips. "I always knew you'd be a good man," she said in words she clearly considered to be the last she would ever say to me. "Nothing could change that . . . nothing."

CHAPTER ELEVEN

On the way back to the valley, I spotted the road that had once led to the Waylord mine and the coal-blackened company town that surrounded it. A wooden sign had been nailed to a tree at the entrance to the road, reminding everyone that although the mine itself had long been shut down, both the mine and the town remained the private property of the Waylord Mining Company.

For all the times I'd swept up the road toward Lila's house, I'd never once turned off it, but Betty Cutler's words suddenly cut through me, *Even after what they done to him at the Waylord mine,* and fired a need in me to discover what had shaped my father, perhaps twisted him, but had, by some transforming means, made him the man she seemed to think I was but the shadow of.

The road into the town was overgrown now, little more than parallel ruts through a snarl of weed, but still maneuverable. Peering down its twisted path, I wondered what it was in my father that Mrs. Cutler so admired, and what had buried it so deeply, I'd never had the slightest glimpse of it for all the years I'd lived within my father's house.

I reached Waylord a few minutes later, got out of my car. A crescent-shaped line of buildings curved around a broad street. The mine lay at the eastern tip of the crescent, a square maw dug out of the hillside. It had been abandoned long ago, of course, along with the company offices and stores.

Just behind the unpainted wooden gate that now blocked the mouth of the mine, I could see the supporting timbers, thick and black, along with the steel roof bolts that held them in place. It was not hard for me to imagine the years during which the mine had been active, the clang of the bell calling the miners to and from the mine, the shuffle of their feet as they passed each other in long lines, clothed in denim coveralls, their heads decked out in plastic helmets and carbide lights.

My father had worked in the Waylord mine from the day he was nine years old, scrambling into the rickety wooden elevator, no doubt peering upward, as miners often do on the descent, drinking in a last greedy gulp of sun before the night engulfed them.

The august offices of the Waylord Mining Company sat on a slight incline, shoved up against the hillside, its wide deck lifted on high wooden stilts. From there, the owners had been able to survey their pinched domain, their mine, their stores, the gray masses who toiled beneath them. I could imagine my father glancing toward them as he filed past, swinging his metal lunch bucket and muttering curses or making jokes at the expense of the rich men who loomed above him, smoking cigars, their thumbs hitched in their suspenders.

"Can I help you with something, mister?"

He wore no uniform, but an unbridled and menacing authority dripped from every pore. Even without the shotgun that hung in the crook of his arm, he would have given off the smoldering sense of what he was. Here standing before me was the mythical gun-thug of my father's grim boyhood, unsmiling, wielding a lawless power to hurt and kill, able to strike terror in all but the strongest hearts.

"This is private property, you know. Posted."

I felt a pinch of fear. "Yes, I know."

"So you saw that sign, did you? Out by the road?"

"I saw it."

He took a step toward me. "Well, in that case, you better be on your way. Like I say. This here land is posted."

I'd already begun to ease back to my car, when another man appeared on the steps of what had once been the company store.

"What's going on, Floyd?" he called.

The gun-thug's shoulders lifted abruptly, like a dog's ears at his master's call. "Oh, it ain't nothing, Mr. Hopper," he yelled back to the old man at the top of the stairs.

"Don't tell me it ain't nothing," the old man snarled. "Who's that feller?" He pointed to me.

The gun-thug looked at me quizzically. "What's your name, mister?" he asked, his tone now suddenly polite, his face hanging slightly, like a scolded puppy.

"Roy Slater," I told him.

"Says his name's Roy Slater," he shouted to the old man.

"Slater?" the old man said in a tone that suggested to me that he recognized the name. "Bring him here, Floyd," he commanded.

A knot formed in my stomach. "Look, I was just . . ."

The gun-thug motioned me toward the old man. "Them stairs . . ." he began.

"Look, I didn't mean to . . ."

The gun-thug peered at me quizzically. "You sick or something?"

"No."

He took this for the truth, turned, and headed for the stairs, motioning me along. "Them stairs," he repeated. "You got to watch how you take 'em. Some's about to give in. Just foller me and you won't fall through."

I followed him up the stairs, carefully avoiding the ones he avoided until we reached the spot where the old man waited, his frame bent like a piece of tin someone had hammered into a misbegotten shape.

"You looking for something here in Waylord?" he asked.

"No, I just wanted to see where my father worked, that's all," I answered. "The Waylord mine, I mean. The hoot-owl shift. That's the one he worked."

The old man grinned. "So he was a night miner." He studied my features. "You say your name's Slater?"

"My father's name is Jesse. Jesse Slater. Did you know him?"

The old man's eyes shot over to the gun-thug. "Floyd. Go on back down to the gate."

The gun-thug nodded slowly, then thudded down the stairs, his great hulk weaving like a wounded bear.

"That boy can't think two steps ahead of hisself," the old man muttered, then turned to me. "You don't look like you're from here. Don't talk like it either."

"I live in California now."

The old man cast his eyes about the dead town almost nostalgically, and the threatening nature of our previous exchange suddenly faded, leaving a soft light in his face. "They ain't nothing left of this place. Used to be lively, though. Name's Hopper. Asa Hopper." He offered his hand.

I shook it. "Glad to meet you."

"Like I said, don't get many visitors up this way."

I looked at him silently for a moment, trying to figure out how to begin, then decided simply to state it flat out. "The truth is, I'm trying to find out something. Just something an old woman said to me once."

"Uh-huh."

"That I'm not the man my father was. I think she said it because my father did something. She mentioned the mine. I got the idea that it must have happened here. Whatever he did."

A silence fell between us, and I could see Hopper's mind turning slowly, dredging the bottom of his long memory. "There ain't nothing to be done about it now, son," he said finally, his tone quiet, measured. "Most of them fellers is long dead. The ones that done it."

I suddenly understood the purpose Hopper thought I must have had in returning to Waylord, the mission he assumed I'd set myself, dear to the heart of all who lived in the hills: vengeance.

"I wasn't planning to do anything to anybody," I assured him. "I just came here to —"

"It was all the talk around here, you know," Hopper said. A grim wonder swam into his eyes. "Nobody figured he'd live, your daddy, but this young feller, a doctor, come up from Kingdom City and tended to him after the beating."

"Why was he beaten?" I asked.

" 'Cause he acted smart," Hopper answered. "Smarted off to 'em. He was just a kid, and all. Sixteen, maybe. Just a kid. So they figured he'd cave in the minute he got spoke to." He nodded. "Right in there. Right by that little candy counter. That's where he smarted off, and that's when they done it.

"Everybody figured it was planned out ahead of time," Hopper went on. " 'Cause them fellers was all standing in different places in the store. When your daddy come in, I mean. Sort of like they was already in position. Waiting for him. The sheriff and them guys that worked for him."

"The sheriff?" I asked. "It was Wallace Porterfield who beat my father up?"

"Him and two more that worked for him," Hopper answered. "Deputies."

I gazed through the dusty glass, surveying the room as Hopper continued, placing the sheriff and his men in the places he indicated. One of them at the front door, a second at the rear, Wallace Porterfield halfway between the two, the massive fulcrum upon whose orders each moved, and finally the store's owner far off to the side, watching it all from behind a stack of cardboard boxes.

"Mr. Warren run the company store back then," the old man said. "Managed the whole thing." He cleared his throat roughly, coughed into his fist. "People said it was Sheriff Porterfield that started it all. Come up to your daddy, sort of put his hand on his shoulder. Said, 'Come with me, boy.' Or something like that."

I saw my father turn to face the enormous granite boulder of Wallace Porterfield, heard him speak the words local legend placed in his mouth.

Where to?
You'll know when you get there.
I ain't going nowhere.
Oh yes you are.
You don't have no right to . . .
I got all the right I need.

"Then Porterfield reached into one of them jars over there," Hopper said. "Took out a piece of penny candy and stuck it right in your daddy's shirt pocket. Looked him right in the eye and said . . ."

You're under arrest, son.
For what?
Stealing candy.

Hopper shook his head. "That's when your daddy smarted off."

You're a liar.

"And he didn't stop with that, your daddy." Hopper's face was fixed in amazement. "He didn't stop. The people in the store heard it all."

And a thief.

"I guess that's when Porterfield noticed how everybody had stopped what they was doing, how they was watching all this. That's when he grabbed your daddy by the arm, but your daddy pulled his arm right out of the sheriff's grip and said some more."

And you're a coward.

In my mind I saw Porterfield's stony glare, the subtle nod he made, then the other two men as they closed in on my father.

"Mr. Warren started rushing everybody out of the store, telling them that he was closing up for a few minutes."

By then they'd surrounded my father, Hopper told me, three gigantic men, peering down at a small bantam rooster of a boy.

"Once Mr. Warren had gotten everybody out of the store, Porterfield and the others took your daddy to a back room," Hopper said.

It came to me in a nightmarish vision, my father dragged into a back room, tormented with jokes and jibes, his slight, wiry frame shoved up against a wall, faces pressed near his, screaming taunts, then the eerie silence before the violence began. I could scarcely imagine how terrified he must have been, how fully his terror must have sucked the life-force out of him, reduced him to a pile of spit and blood faster than he could possibly have dreamed it before the beating began, his swollen eyes barely able to make out the polished shoes of the men who towered over him when it was over, laughing as they poked the tips of their boots at his ribs, trying to rouse him just enough to have another go, puffing blue smoke into the fetid air, finally giving up, filing out.

"They all come out a few minutes later. People seen one of the deputies flicking his hand, like it was numb. Porterfield had pulled his jacket off, rolled up his sleeves. He was dabbing at a stain on his shirt with a handkerchief. They heard something too, the people outside. Heard Porterfield look back into the store, to where Mr. Warren was still settin' at the counter. Heard him say something like 'Don't worry, Henry, that boy's lovin' days are over.' " He shrugged. "People never was clear on why they done it to him," Hopper told me. "I mean, he didn't steal nothing. Wasn't bothering nobody in the store."

Wallace Porterfield's voice sounded like a heavy bell in my mind: *Don't worry, Henry, that boy's loving days are over.* "Deidre," I said almost to myself. "It was over Henry Warren's daughter."

Hopper shook his head. "Well, if that's so, he sure must have cared a whole lot about that girl to take a beating like that."

"Yes, he did," I said softly, imagining how broken my father must have been, groaning on the floor as Wallace Porterfield stood over him, and yet able, too, to imagine him rising from that same assault, determined and unbowed, something at the fleshy core of him turning into steel. "But I'm still surprised it stopped him from seeing her."

Hopper scratched at his jaw. "Well, he didn't have no chance to see her. 'Cause Mr. Warren shipped her off not long after that. Out of Kingdom County. To one of them schools they got up north. You know, where kids live at school." He shrugged. "Anyway, she never come back to Waylord. Nor Kingdom County neither, far as I know. Nobody never seen her around here again."

I saw her, a teenage girl hustled into the back of a car, her father at the wheel, starting the engine, pulling away, Deidre glancing back toward a town she'd never see again, hills in the distance where a boy lay half dead in a mountain hovel, battered, nearly broken, a boy whose loving days, at her departure, were surely and forever over.

So that was it, I thought as I walked down

the stairs to my car a few minutes later. I'd solved the mystery of my father's unhappiness, found the lost love for which he'd pined through all the years. He'd loved Deidre Warren and for her sake had taken a beating that I knew in the end would not have stopped him, something Henry Warren must have known as well, something Wallace Porterfield, for all his confidence in violent intimidation, must ultimately have told him. *There's no stopping that boy,* so that they'd finally spirited Deidre Warren away, taken her to where my father, for all the determination of his will, would never be able to reach her.

For a very brief moment, I reveled in the solution to my father's mystery, pleased, more or less intellectually, to have uncovered it. Then, like an intruder in the night, something dark encroached upon my reverie, the terrible truth that that long-ago beating had not only marked my father, wounded and distorted him, but that ultimately it had done the same to our relationship. For how cowardly and pathetic he must have viewed my response to Porterfield's son many years later, the way I'd done nothing in the face of the insult he'd shouted at Lila on the mountain road. And for all its horror and devastation, how strangely heroic my father must have seen Archie's doomed attempt to run away with Gloria Kellogg.

So now I knew why, even in my adulthood,

I had never seemed a man to my father. It was not my education or my job that condemned me. It was the fact that at the critical moment I had not fought for love, but had merely turned away, let Lonnie Porterfield's insult stand, even made up a limp excuse for his cruelty, *He was young, Dad. He was drunk,* then done nothing to avenge what he had said to Lila, the rape his words must have seemed to her, and by that miserable weakness and failure marked myself forever as worthless.

That you can never gain your father's admiration, nor even his respect, is the darkest thing a son may know, and as I headed down the mountain that afternoon, I knew it to the full. I might escape the iron grip of Waylord, become in all worlds renowned, but *Pitiful, Roy, pitiful* was an indictment I would never be able to escape.

PART II

(HAPTER TWELVE

Life deals the cards facedown.

That was a phrase that often returned to me during the next weeks of that summer.

It was my freshman English teacher who'd said it in class one day. What do all writers eventually tell us, he'd asked, then stared out over his students, a field of blank faces. Simply this, he said, answering his own question: life deals the cards facedown.

So much so, as I later learned, that even as the cards are turned, some part remains hidden, like the half-smile on the jack of hearts.

For nearly six weeks after leaving the Waylord mine that afternoon I occupied myself almost exclusively in the daily physical tasks of caring for my father — cleaning, washing, chores that used up time and kept me out of his sight. I cooked what he called his "three squares," and took them to his room, where he ate alone, if he ate, the plate in his lap, the television blaring. As often as possible I took my own meals outside the house, usually at the Crispy Cone in Kingdom City. When at home I sequestered myself in my room, the door closed, books scattered about, providing another world into which I immediately retreated at the sound of my father's tread outside my door.

I felt no pity for him. I knew what he thought of me, and so I returned a judgment just as harsh, brooded on how little he'd made of his life, how dry and loveless he was, a crude old man who deserved even less than he'd gotten. It is a freezing thing to know that you can never rise in your parents' estimation, that something at the very core of you fills them with contempt, and after Waylord I lived in that icy world, giving my father as little as I could, caring for him as I would have cared for a dog, though with less affection, and no joy, waiting in anxious anticipation for his approaching death.

Even when we talked, I kept our conversation limited to the most inconsequential matters. Archie disappeared from my conversation, as did my mother. Waylord vanished as well. There was no more talk of Lila. Betty Cutler ceased to be, along with Deidre Warren. Since I was no longer involved with Lonnie Porterfield, he also fell out of our discourse, along with his father, though I sometimes saw them both, Lonnie striding down the main street of Kingdom City, the old sheriff seated like an aging potentate beneath the large oak that shaded his vast lawn.

I had banished all these people from my

life, banished them along with my father, determined that I would never again let any one of them cast even the most trivial judgment on my character or the nature of my life. I wanted to erase them like chalk from a board. For a time I even believed I had.

Then, on a bright Sunday morning, when I was sitting in my bed, I heard my father tramp down the corridor, and seconds later the rap of his knuckles on my door.

"Come in," I said dryly.

The door opened, and to my astonishment, he stood before me, fully dressed in a shiny black suit, shaved for the first time in more than a week, his sagging face slick and glistening in the morning light, his body reeking of aftershave.

"Juanita died," my father said in a tone that was incongruously cheerful. "You know, that old Indian up in Waylord."

"Juanita Her-Many-Horses," I said, remembering the last time I'd seen her, a ragged old lady seated on cinder blocks, fanning herself with a mortuary fan.

"That's the one. Found her yesterday. Laying in a pigpen. Been there for days. Damn old pig ate some of her."

"How do you know all this?"

"Heard it on the radio," my father answered. "They're burying her today. Had to do it fast, I guess, 'cause of the shape she was in." He ran his fingers down the lapel of his jacket. "Figured I'd spruce up and go to the funeral."

He made a slow turn, like an aged dancer, shrunken but not entirely graceless in his scarecrow suit. "What do you think?"

When I didn't answer, he cocked his head to the left, glimpsed himself in the mirror on my bureau, regarded himself approvingly. "They's always lots a females at a funeral, you know. I'm not that bad-looking for a feller that's dying." He fingered the cracked brown belt that held his trousers. "Fact is, that's the best thing about me. From a woman's point of view, I mean. That I ain't gonna be around that long."

"You're not serious, are you?"

He laughed. "Not about courting," he said lightly, his tone still oddly bright. "But I'd like to go to Juanita's funeral."

"I didn't think you knew her."

"I didn't know her all that well," he admitted, "but I thought I might see Betty Cutler. They was close, her and Juanita. She'll be at Juanita's funeral. Figured I'd say hi, you know, one last time." His eyes glinted softly, and in them I could see the fading sunlight of his days. "You'd drive me up there if I asked you to, wouldn't you, Roy?"

I had no desire to return to Waylord, to see Betty Cutler or Lila, and yet, for the first time in weeks, I did feel something, though perhaps it was nothing more than acknowledgment of the inexplicable hold our fathers have over us no matter how much we wish to escape it.

"All right," I said with a shrug. "I'll drive you up there."

"Funeral's at eleven," he told me. "We should probably be on the way by ten."

He turned to leave the room, then stopped, and shifted around to face me once again. "I done something, you know. Done it this morning while you was sleeping. Something I 'spect you might be interested in. Come here, I'll show you."

I reluctantly rose from my bed and followed him.

"There it is," he said when we reached the kitchen.

He pointed to a gallon jug on the table. At the bottom of the jug, several cockroaches spun about madly, antennae frantically probing the glass wall, seeking a way out.

"I'm starting with five of them," my father said. "If I outlive all five, then I'll get me some more." He saw the puzzled look on my face. "It's like an experiment," he explained. "Science." He picked up the jug and turned it toward me. "See, I poked airholes in the lid there. Sprinkled sugar and water on the bottom of the jar. Figured that ought to give them enough to eat and drink. You know, for a normal life."

"A normal life? In a jar?"

"Well, it ain't no better for them on the outside. Matter of fact, it's probably a lot worse. What with birds after them all the time, and snakes. Hell, they don't have to worry about them things inside the jar."

"They're insects, Dad. I don't think *worry* enters into it."

He returned the jug to its place on top of the refrigerator. "Anyway, I'm gonna keep 'em in the shade, make 'em nice and comfortable. It's cool up there. They'll enjoy it. Living in that jar."

"What's this all about, Dad? This experiment?"

He looked curiously exposed, like someone who'd inadvertently revealed a small portion of himself that he'd long kept concealed. "I had an interest, you know," he said. "Things in general, I guess. Science, you might call it. Read a book or two about how things work. How things is put together. They had this school they was building just over the county line. Sort of a science school I heard about. So I figured I might —" He stopped, thought better of what he'd intended to say, then retreated into a grin and headed for the refrigerator. "Hell, I'll set 'em loose," he said.

"No, don't," I told him not only quickly but with a quickening, a small surge of feeling not for my father, but for the ghostly boy his words had conjured up. "We'll keep an eye on them."

"Conduct an experiment," my father said, watching me closely. "Ain't that how you say it?"

"Yes, it is."

He smiled. "Okay, Roy, we'll conduct us an experiment."

I made bacon, eggs, even a portion of the red-eye gravy I remembered him liking when I was a boy. It was little more than grease and bits of bacon, but he sopped it up with relish.

"Mighty good," he said after he'd raked his biscuit through the last of it. "Mighty good, Roy." He wiped his mouth with the dishcloth he used for a napkin, downed what was left of his coffee, then pushed his plate away and got to his feet. "Let me know when you're ready to go."

I spent the next hour reading in the chair beside the window, glancing out occasionally to observe the withered garden my father had planted, then abandoned. Several years before, he'd gathered my mother's clothes and burned them in a pile as ragged and disordered as his marriage. I'd watched him as he'd poked the smoldering mound with a crooked stick. I would not have given him another year of life back then, but he'd staggered on, as if determined to prove just how little nourishment his soul required. If that were true, then I wondered if this same bleak goal might be my true inheritance, not my father's withered garden, nor his worthless house, but the grim feat of showing just how little a man needed to survive.

He was waiting by the car when I came out at ten sharp. He'd changed his appearance slightly since breakfast, added black shoes to the ensemble, not exactly polished, but wiped with a wet cloth. He'd changed his tie so that it now hung like a thin red snake, its arrowhead tail dangling a full three inches above his belt buckle. A heart-shaped tie clasp held it in place, the one part of his attire I'd never seen before.

"Well?" he asked as he got to his feet. "Do I look good enough to go courting?"

"It's a funeral," I reminded him. "Not a dance."

He shrugged. "In Waylord them two gets mixed together." He turned toward the stairs, his gaze suddenly caught on the old brown Ford he'd driven for the past twelve years, a dusty relic whose odometer topped a hundred thousand cheerless miles.

"Would you prefer to drive?" I asked as I stepped up beside him.

"Naw," he said. "Naw," he repeated. "You better do it. I guess my driving days is over." It was the first time I'd heard him actually give in to the fact of his imminent dependency.

As we headed along the valley roads, my

146

father kept his eyes fixed straight ahead, hardly giving a second glance to the world he'd lived in for so many years. He paid no attention to the farmhouses we swept by, nor the fields and woods that surrounded them.

A mile or so up the road, we passed the house where Archie had done it. A large metal mailbox proclaimed that the Tompkins family now occupied the spacious rooms through which the Kelloggs had once moved with such certainty that they were safe, protected by law and social standing and friends in high places, never imagining that it could all be blown away in a few murderous seconds.

There were children in the yard as we drove by, a little boy and girl, the boy around eight years old, the girl no more than six. They were darting playfully over the neatly cut grass, kicking at a red-striped ball, crying excitedly as the ball hurled toward the road. *Get it, get it, get it.*

My father glanced at them as we drifted by, and for a moment seemed to see Christmas holly curled around the black mailbox, snow begin to fall softly as it had that night. He released a ragged breath, then turned away, locking his eyes on the road ahead.

He didn't appear to take note of anything else until we turned onto the red clay roads that twined upward, finally reached Bishop's

Gap, then moved ever higher into the hills. At that point his gaze began to shift about, noting this house or that one, a dell here, a stream there. From time to time he even went so far as to make a comment about the long-past resident of some ramshackle farmhouse. "Old Man Stuckley used to live there," he'd say, or "Maude Cowper kept bees over yonder. She always brought a jar of honeycomb when she went visiting."

When we reached the old mining road, I nodded and said, "Down there's where we found Clayton Spivey."

We drove on awhile in silence, then my father said, "Did you ever find out much about him, Roy?"

"Just that he was lonely," I answered. "No wife or kids. Not even any friends."

"Never found no balance."

"Balance?"

"Something my daddy used to tell me," my father said. "That's a point where things seem about as good as they can get. When there ain't nothing weighing too heavy on the wrong side of things. That's what we should look for, he said, this here balance."

I glanced over to him. "Did you ever find it?"

He lowered his eyes slightly. "Never even got close," he said. "According to the radio, they're having the funeral at the Holiness Church. Same church Betty's husband went

148

to. Buford was his name. A helpless little feller, Betty said. But nice enough."

I wanted to say nothing, ask no further question, but my need to explore this old corner of my father's life lit the very candle I thought I'd snuffed out.

"You must have known her pretty well, then," I said. "For her to tell you something like that. About her husband. What he was like. Something so . . . intimate."

My father caught the hint of an insinuation in my tone, but dismissed it.

"Marriage don't close a woman's mouth, Roy. Or nothing else, for that matter. If you'd ever been married, you'd know that. Anyway, I never screwed Betty Cutler, if that's what you're getting at. We was never nothing more than friends. You think just 'cause we talked, we had to be screwing?"

"I have no way of knowing."

He eyed me closely, hit the mark. "You ain't never been friends with a woman, have you, Roy? Just friends, and nothing else?"

The answer pained me, but I gave it anyway. "No, not really."

"How about men? You got any buddies out there in California?"

I remembered the rawboned men who'd stood in ragged circles about town, the way they'd parted to receive my father with a clap on the shoulders or a mute, respectful nod, these pulpwood haulers and timbermen I'd seen as little more than work-animals in their dusty overalls and floppy hats. More than anything, I'd wanted to avoid the crude manual labor that had defined their lives. But did some part of me also want to be like them? For they'd had an easy way with one another, as well as a deep competence with physical things. They could tear apart and reassemble engines, mend roofs, build sheds and fences, and I knew that they could truly respect only other men who could do the same.

"Just people I work with," I admitted. "I wouldn't call them . . . buddies."

My father didn't say it outright, but I knew what he was thinking. That no matter how unbalanced his life had been, it had never been so bereft as mine, solitary, friendless, a teacher of children who were not my own, surrounded by interchangeable acquaintances, a life lived by the sea, among strangers, in a world where blood was truly no thicker than water.

"Must be mighty nice out there in California, then," he said. "If you can like it without a friend."

"I don't like it," I told him, speaking with a sudden surprising candor. "It's just where I ended up."

My father's gaze turned toward me. "Well, the house is yours if you ever want to come back to Kingdom County."

I shook my head. "I won't be coming back to Kingdom County."

"Sell it, then," he said dryly, without the slightest hint of sentiment for the old place. "Won't bring much, but ain't nobody else to give it to."

There were only a few people inside the church, all of them gathered in the first few pews, staring at Juanita's plain wooden coffin, the handful of wildflowers, stems tied with a white ribbon, that rested on top of it. Betty Cutler sat in the front pew, her gray hair wound into a bun and neatly pinned behind her head. Lila sat beside her in a plain black dress.

My father and I took seats at the back of the church, listened as the preacher said the usual things. After that, a straggling line of people moved down the center aisle, Lila in the lead, holding her mother close at her side.

She caught sight of me as she neared the back of the church, nodded, then moved by, guiding her mother down the front stairs and out to the cemetery.

"Lila's still mighty pretty, ain't she?" my father whispered.

"Yes, she is."

A final prayer was offered at the graveside, then the coffin was lowered into the ground. Lila and her mother stood together, watching silently as the brown casket sank slowly into the earth. Then Lila bent forward, grasped a crust of dry sod, and tossed it into the grave.

Through it all my father held his gaze on Betty Cutler, almost wistfully, as I noticed, the past pouring over him like a glistening falls.

Lila took her mother's arm and led her over to where we stood.

"Hi, Roy," she said. "Hello, Mr. Slater."

"I was sorry to hear about Juanita," my father said. "How-do, Betty."

Mrs. Cutler squinted. "Who's that?"

"It's Jesse," my father answered. "Jesse Slater."

She looked as if she'd been hit by a ray of light. "Well, I'm born again."

My father smiled. "How'd you like to take a little stroll, Betty?" he asked, his voice so bright and youthful, I glimpsed the vibrant young man he must once have been.

Mrs. Cutler gave no answer, but my father must have caught something in her gaze, for he stepped over briskly, took her arm, tucked it beneath his own, and drew her away from Lila and me. For a moment I watched them silently, helplessly, in admiration of my father's way with a woman, how firm his stride was, how sure his touch, with what ease he'd drawn Betty Cutler back into the circle of his affection.

"Roy?"

It was Lila's voice, and the sound of it was

like a trumpet in my mind.

"I didn't expect to see you again," she said.

"My father wanted to come to Juanita's funeral," I told her.

"He knew Juanita?"

"Not very well. He said he came because he wanted to see your mother. Tell her good-bye."

Lila glanced out over the cemetery to where my father and Betty Cutler had come to a halt at a small stone near the gnarled trunk of a dogwood.

"Your father always seemed so nice," she said. "So gentle."

We watched the old man as he knelt slowly, brushed his hand across the top of the squat gray stone, then peered up at Lila's mother, who turned away.

"He's not gentle. Just old and sick."

A cloud moved across Lila's face. For a moment, she struggled to keep silent, struggled so hard that when the words finally broke from her, I'd expected them to hit like small exploding shells. But they fell softly instead. "What's the matter, Roy? You seem so . . ."

My father's judgment burst resentfully from my mouth. "Pitiful?"

She looked as surprised by the word as the bitter tone with which I'd pronounced it.

"No, not pitiful," she said. "Alone."

I released a brittle laugh. "Well, that's certainly true." Then, before she could say more, I added, "I didn't want that much, you know. When I was a kid. It strikes me sometimes just how little I wanted." The words flooded out now. "I guess I must have seemed ambitious to you. Full of big ideas. Go to college. All that. But I really didn't want that much, Lila. Just a simple life. Nothing great, nothing grand. Just a simple life."

Lila started to speak, but I lifted my hand.

"A family," I blurted out, my tone unexpectedly wounded. "Kids."

She stared at me with a terrible stillness. "Maybe I wanted that too," she said. "But I couldn't, Roy, because I knew —" She stopped suddenly.

"Knew what?"

I could see something rising in her, a long-caged animal clawing to get out.

"That it couldn't be, Roy," she said. "Not after the murders."

"After the murders."

Three days after the murders, I'd driven to Lila's house. By then Archie was dead and I'd come to tell her about the funeral, expecting her to join me at my brother's grave. But Betty Cutler had met me at the door, told me that Lila had fallen ill, that she was sleeping, that I should stay away for another few days or so. Her final words rang in my ears: *She'll be all right in time.*

"What did the murders have to do with us?" I asked.

She lifted her hand. "I can't bear this, Roy," she said.

"Did you think that I —"

"I can't, Roy," she repeated, then, like someone broken on the wheel, she turned and walked away.

CHAPTER THIRTEEN

I mentioned nothing of what had happened between Lila and me as I drove my father back down the mountain road a few minutes later. Instead, I brooded mutely, playing the scene over and over in my head, the way Lila had turned away from me.

My father watched me silently, his own mood growing steadily darker, the lightness that had touched him earlier in the day now leeching away like something fading in the sun.

After a time, he drew a pack of cigarettes from his jacket pocket. "There ain't much left of Betty."

"People get old."

"It ain't just that." He lit the cigarette, waved out the match. "She's weighed down by how things turned out for Lila."

"What did she tell you about Lila?"

He blew a column of smoke from the corner of his mouth. "Just that nothing ever worked out for her. I told her, I said, Well, Betty, fact is you can't do nothing about what happens to your kids. You git the kids you git, and that's what you end up with."

Meaning, of course, that he had ended up

with me, a card dealt to him facedown.

"That works both ways, of course," I said curtly. "You don't pick your parents either."

He didn't respond, and in the following silence the old isolation slowly descended upon him, so that he finally assumed the stricken appearance I hadn't seen since the night following Archie's funeral. A rage had roared through him for days by then, one that had finally dissolved into a solitary muteness, so that he'd ceased railing against my mother and me, against Horace Kellogg and Gloria, the "puny little thing" who'd caused it all. Finally, at sunrise, he'd poured himself a whiskey, the only drink I'd ever seen him take, and sat, sipping it silently, the darkness in his eyes draining light from the dawning air.

The same isolation gripped him now.

"Pore old Betty," he said. "She had a good heart. Helped me with this girl I knew once. We was going to run off. Me and this girl. Betty was gonna pick her up and bring her back up to Waylord." He drew in a long breath, his eyes sweeping over to the granite precipice known locally as Dawson Rock. "Waited for her right around here, as a matter of fact. But her old man got wind of it somehow. I shouldn't have waited like I done. When I seen she wasn't coming, I should have gone and got her and took her away. Would have saved a world of trouble if I'd done that."

A world of trouble — meaning the whole dreary life that had come to him after that, the one he had inflicted on Archie and me.

A fist squeezed my stomach, a wave of resentment that he'd gotten all the things I'd most deeply wanted in my life, a wife, children, but that he'd squandered it all by brooding on a teenage romance, or on the beating he'd taken for it, and thus driven away whatever love had been offered him after that.

"Yeah, you should have gone after that girl and taken her away," I said scathingly. "It would have saved us all a lot of trouble if you'd done that. Mama. Archie. Me."

He heard the angry tone in my voice, turned away, and peered at the edge of the cliff. "Nothing could have saved you trouble, Roy."

"What do you mean by that?"

He shrugged silently.

"What do you mean?" I demanded. "What do you mean that nothing could have saved me trouble?"

He turned toward me sharply. " 'Cause you like it, Roy. Being a 'troubled' person. Like it shows you're smart."

"You're nuts," I snapped, honing in on my father now, stalking him like a prizefighter, pressing him toward the ropes. "You don't know me. You've never tried to know me. You never did anything with me. Never even talked to me except in that insulting way of yours. Never tried to teach me anything or to —"

"Hold it right there," my father fired back. "Am I hearing this right? You think I never tried to teach you nothing, Roy? My God, everything I did, there was a lesson in it."

"What lesson?"

"The only one there is. To do the right thing."

A derisive laugh broke from me. "The right thing?" I frantically sought a way to hit back hard, fell him with a single brutal punch. "That was the lesson in what you did to Scooter?" I saw the pistol pass from my father's hand to Archie's. "What you made Archie do to him?"

"You don't think there was a lesson in that?"

"There was nothing but cruelty in it," I said. "Cruelty, Dad. To Archie and to Scooter both."

"Well, you never run off again, did you?" my father demanded hotly. "You never took Archie off with you again. A boy that never had a mind of his own, was always under your thumb, would do whatever you told him to. You never led him off again after Scooter."

"No, I didn't, but . . ."

"That was the real lesson, Roy. That's why I handed that pistol to Archie instead of you.

Made him do it instead of you."

The first bullet spun through the void. Scooter's body jerked to the right. A panicked howl split the air.

"I was trying to teach you something by making Archie do it," my father said.

A second bullet. Again the spotted flanks jerked. A bloody leg buckled.

"You know what I was trying to teach, Roy? Plenty of things."

The shots came one after the other in a slow, torturous rhythm. Archie squeezing the trigger each time my father commanded, *Again, again, again.*

"That you need to think before you get somebody caught up in something. That you need to think of what might happen to them. Because if you don't, that other person might get hurt. Somebody you didn't intend to hurt. Like Archie didn't think Scooter could get hurt because he run off with you."

A final shot rang out, loud, deafening, reverberating through the overhanging hills, and Scooter at last lay dead.

"And like you didn't think that Archie could be hurt by you running off and taking him with you. Well, they both got hurt, Roy. Scooter got kilt, and Archie was the one I made kill him. But the lesson was for you."

I glared at him furiously. "Bullshit."

"It's the truth, Roy. The fact is Archie wasn't smart enough to get nobody into trouble. But you was. You was the smart one. That's why the lesson was for you. So you wouldn't be so quick to get people took up in stuff that might get them hurt. Archie would have done anything you told him to. 'Cause he loved you, Roy. And if somebody loves you, you can hurt 'em bad. Believe me, there ain't nobody knows that more'n me."

I stared into my father's emaciated face, and suddenly knew what that whole bloody lesson had really been about.

"It was Deidre Warren," I said. "That's who you hurt." Hopper's voice sounded in my brain: *She never come back to Waylord. Nobody never seen Deidre around again.* "What happened to Deidre?"

My father's eyes softened. "Never mind."

"She never came back to Kingdom County," I added. "Where did she go?"

"I told you, forget it."

"I don't want to forget it."

My father released a weary breath. "Baltimore, if you got to know. That's where she went. Some school up there. Cold damn day her old man took her. She was all bundled up."

"You saw her go?"

"Seen Old Man Warren walk her to the car. Guess he'd already set it up to get her out of Kingdom County. She didn't look right. Face looked bruised. Figure he must have hit her, Old Man Warren." His voice

161

hardened. "Porterfield was there too. Had his hand on Deidre's shoulder. Put her right in the front seat of his car and drove off with her."

I saw Deidre's scared white face peer out of the rear window of Porterfield's car as it drew away, leaving smeared tracks in the snow.

"Nothing I could do about it," my father said. "Car was pulling out already. I was too banged up to run after it." He shook his head. "Planned to go after her. Took a job there at the pulpwood factory. Figured I'd save up. But by the time I done that, it was too late."

"Why was it too late?"

" 'Cause she died," he answered quietly, and his face took on an inexpressible tenderness. "Took sick at that school Old Man Warren sent her off to." He pinned his eyes on the road, though he seemed to regard nothing that lay before him. "She'd still be alive if she'd stayed clear of me."

He said nothing else as we headed out of the hills and into the valley, a noonday heat now bearing down upon us, so that even with the car windows wide open I felt as if we were locked in a sweltering cage. And yet, I sensed that the real heat remained inside my father, a slow, destructive fire that had never stopped burning. By the time we reached home, he seemed little more than ash.

CHAPTER FOURTEEN

I remained in the car, and watched as my father made his way up the stairs and into the house, switching lights on and off as he moved through its steamy interior. In the kitchen he walked to the refrigerator, drew down the jar, shook it slightly, then peered inside, a Waylord scientist in his shiny pants.

After that I pulled back onto the road and drove around for hours, replaying my last meeting with Lila, remembering the terrible sadness that had overwhelmed her after the murders. Something had gone out in her that night. On my last night in Kingdom County, we sat in my old Chevy, without touching, the passion she'd once shown me entirely drained away. And now I remembered the look in Lila's eyes on the day my bus pulled away — all too similar to the look in Sheriff Porterfield's, the same suspicion playing darkly in her mind.

But why?

The question circled insistently in my mind. I knew that Lila could not have known anything about the murders. I had told her nothing. Archie had told her nothing. She'd never spoken to Gloria again, and of course,

Horace and Lavenia Kellogg were dead.

So what did she know, I wondered, that had changed everything, destroyed all our plans, and finally caused her to write the letter I'd later thrown into the sea, *I can't marry you, Roy. Don't come back for me.*

It was nearly eight in the evening when the pinch of hunger finally overtook my long brooding. I knew that my father had already retired to his bed, so I pulled into the Crispy Cone before returning to the house.

It was a squat, cement building, garishly lit, with a checkered linoleum floor that blearily reflected the long fluorescent lights above it. At the counter, I ordered a hamburger, fries, and coffee, then took a seat at one of the booths that ran alongside the front window.

My order came a few minutes later, brought by a freckled-faced boy in a wrinkled uniform, a paper cap resting uneasily on his head.

"Three," he said.

I looked at him quizzically.

"Your order number," the boy added dully.

I glanced at the paper receipt half crumpled in my hand. "Oh, yeah, right."

He placed the plate on the table before me. "Thanks for eating at Crispy Cone."

I ate slowly, stalling for time, dreading the moment when I would have to return, lie in the dark, turn toward the window, and see Lila's face reflected in the glass, all memory

164

of her, the long summer days, the times we'd made love beside Jessup Creek, all of that now stained by the grim half-light of our last encounter, sealed in the dark chamber of Lila's cryptic words:

Because I knew . . .

I finished the sentence myself.

. . . that you were there.

The jukebox started up suddenly, and I turned toward it.

At the far end of the room, two teenage couples jostled about playfully, the girls giggling shyly, the boys winking to each other and shifting restlessly in their seats. Twenty years before, it might have been Lila and me in that same booth, facing Archie and Gloria, all of us on yet another double date, just back from the movie house in Kingdom City.

We'd gone out together perhaps thirty times, just four high school kids, nothing to take note of, and certainly nothing to fear.

By then Horace Kellogg had realized that Gloria was not just dating Archie, but that she'd fallen in love with him.

I'd first learned of the change on a chilly September night as Archie sat disconsolately on the side of his bed. "Mr. Kellogg says I got to stop seeing Gloria. Says we're moving too fast, her and me."

"What does Gloria think?" I asked.

"She says we should run away and get married and not pay no attention to what her daddy says."

"Where does that leave you, Arch?"

"I don't know, Roy. What do you think about it? Us running off, I mean."

I knew that Archie undoubtedly lacked the necessary skills to plan and execute anything even remotely as complicated as eloping with Horace Kellogg's daughter, so I said, "I think Mr. Kellogg will probably simmer down after a while."

"No," my brother told me. "He won't, Roy."

Now, watching the boys across the room, I marveled that I had not taken my brother's grim certainty more seriously.

It was only an hour later, Lila now with me in the car, listening as I related what Archie had told me, that I realized just how serious the situation might become.

"I think he's going to do it, Roy," she said. "I think he's going to run off with Gloria."

I looked over at her and fairly swooned at how luminous her face appeared in the car's darkened interior.

"Once he starts it, he won't know how to stop," she added, her voice grave, like one who'd already glimpsed what was to come, my brother's car lurching along the tall

166

hedges that bordered the Kelloggs' newly paved driveway, gray footprints in the path that led from his car to the white door, the way that door opened slowly to reveal Lavenia Kellogg's doomed face.

The teenagers rose and made their way out to the parking lot. There they gathered briefly beside a light blue Ford, the Crispy Cone's flashing sign winking brightly in its shiny chrome grille.

Through the restaurant's window I watched them talking, the two boys still at each other playfully, bobbing and weaving, the girls giggling wildly, all of them utterly carefree and unselfconscious, youth like a blindfold wrapped around their eyes.

They piled into the car a few minutes later, driving away quickly, tossing gravel behind the whirling tires to leave a curving trail behind them that tormented me like the one I'd left behind so long ago, two gray lines through the freshly fallen snow that had covered the road past Horace Kellogg's house.

"You finished?"

I glanced toward the voice, high and reedy, of the woman who stood above me, her apron stained with ketchup, mustard, cooking oil.

"I'll take your plate if you're finished," she said, already reaching for the plate, so that the metal name tag on her uniform glinted in the cruel fluorescent light, drawing me away from what Archie had later done that night, returning me to what I had done instead.

"Porterfield," I said.

She looked at me quizzically. "Do I know you?"

"You're Lonnie Porterfield's daughter, aren't you?"

"Yes, sir."

In the red uniform, with a small paper cap pinned to her hair, she looked even younger than her years, which I guessed at about fourteen.

"My name's Slater. Roy Slater. Your father and I went to high school together."

"Oh yeah, I heard him mention you at home. You were with him when ya'll found that dead guy in the woods. My name's Jackie. Nice to meet you."

"I've been here a few times," I told her. "But I've never seen you here before."

"I usually work the morning shift, that's probably why," Jackie said. "But Sue got sick, so I had to come in for her tonight." She glanced about warily, as if determining if the coast was clear, then slid into the seat opposite me. "You're the one from California, right? Been out there a long time, my daddy said."

"A very long time."

She studied me a moment. "Like I said, Daddy was talking about you. How you was helping him find out about that fellow you found dead." Her eyes widened. "Did you see his face?"

"Yes."

"All bloody?"

"There was some blood."

Jackie cringed. "My daddy sees stuff like that all the time, but it makes me woozy." One hand leisurely scratched the other, pink nails drawing white lines across her pale flesh. "I can't look at that kind of stuff."

A sharp laugh broke from her. "Imagine me up there with you and Daddy. I'd have been barfing all over the place." She glanced about the restaurant again. "I'm not supposed to talk to customers."

"Then maybe you shouldn't."

But she paid no mind to this. "Can I ask you something? Do you live in Hollywood?"

"No. I live in northern California."

She was clearly disappointed to hear it. "What brings you back to Kingdom County?"

"My father's dying."

Jackie's eyes registered no response. "They make movies about people that go to Hollywood to be in the movies," she added. "So, how come you went out there?"

"College," I said.

"I'm going to college. Kingdom Community. Soon as I graduate high school. I'm going to study hotel management. I was thinking about California. They've got lots of hotels out there."

She looked at me quizzically. "Have you ever been to Hollywood?"

"No, I haven't."

Once again, she took this in her stride. "What happened anyway? To that guy ya'll found. He was dead already when you got there, Daddy said."

"He had a disease," I told her.

"Like a heart attack or something?"

"More or less."

"You didn't know the guy?"

"I never met him."

She offered a quick "Hmm," then added, "But you knew the woman that came down to identify him. That's what Daddy said."

"We went to school together."

Jackie's eyes lit briefly on something over my shoulder, then returned to me, bright with a shrewd intuition. "Did ya'll date, that woman and you?"

"Yes, we did."

"My daddy wants me to date boys that go to the community college. Not these boys around here." She gave me a conspiratorial wink. "But I don't always do that. Sometimes I even go over to Busters. That's where the local boys hang out." She laughed. "It's okay as long as my granddaddy don't find out about it." She lowered her voice slightly. "Long time ago he was the sheriff of Kingdom County."

"I know," I said. "But why wouldn't you be more concerned about your father finding out about your going over to Busters?"

She laughed. "Daddy? He don't have no control over me. Never has."

"But your grandfather does?"

Something darkened in her eyes. "He ain't to be crossed, my granddaddy."

"But he's an old man. What could he —"

"Plenty," Jackie said. "He could do plenty. And he would too. Granddaddy can't stand them boys over at Busters. Says they're trash. If he found out I was dating one of them, he'd fix him good."

Make sure his loving days were over, I thought.

She smiled brightly again. "You know, I heard my daddy and my granddaddy talking about you. About how you was helping Daddy out. My granddaddy said they wasn't no use in having you look into it 'cause you'd be on her side. If it turned out that feller was shot or something. And that woman done it. The one you dated. My granddaddy said you wouldn't help out on that, 'cause you owed her a favor."

"I don't think your grandfather could know anything about me," I said. "Or any . . . woman."

"Oh, I bet he could," she said confidently, standing her ground. "Back when he was sheriff, Granddaddy knew everything that went on in Kingdom County. He told my daddy she'd saved you a world of trouble one time and that was a favor you had to pay back."

"I can't imagine what he was talking about," I said.

CHAPTER FIFTEEN

Doc Poole was on the way to his car when I pulled into the driveway later that night, lugging the same battered bag he'd brought to my mother's bedside during her final illness.

"Evening, Roy," he said as I got out of my car. "I was just looking in on Jesse. He's not doing very well, is he?"

"He rallied a little this morning," I told him. "But it didn't last."

"He doesn't want me to check on him anymore." He slapped his hat softly against his leg. "I figured he'd come to that conclusion when he didn't show up for his appointment this afternoon."

"I didn't know he had an appointment."

"He didn't want you to know, I guess."

"He's ready to die," I said.

Doc Poole nodded. "Yeah. To tell you the truth, he was lucky to have had the time he did, considering what they did to him when he was a boy."

I remembered what Asa Hopper had told me before, that a young doctor had come up from Kingdom City, treated my father as best he could.

"So it was you," I said. "You were the

young doctor who came up to Waylord after the beating."

"That was the first time I ever saw Jesse. Didn't think he'd make it. I really didn't." He paused a moment, regarding me closely, then added, "You've had your share of trouble, too. That terrible thing with Archie."

I suddenly saw something in the old doctor's eyes.

"You came to see Archie that last night," I said. "I passed you in the corridor as I was leaving."

Doc Poole yanked a handkerchief from his back pocket and swabbed his neck. "Yeah, I looked in on him. But when I left, I didn't have any inkling what Archie was going to do, did you? It's hard to kill yourself that way."

I shook my head. "When I left he told me that he'd see me in the blackberry patch."

"That was all?" Doc Poole asked.

"Yes."

This brief answer seemed to satisfy a gnawing question. "Well, I'd better be going. Good night, Roy. Let me know if I can be of any help."

He'd already gone a few steps before I drew him back with a question. "Did something happen that night? Between you and Archie?"

Doc Poole hesitated a moment, an old man trained in keeping confidences. "No, nothing happened between Archie and me," he replied. "But Sheriff Porterfield said something strange when I left that night, and I always wondered if he mentioned it to you." He looked oddly pained, as if something had long ago caught in his soul, a tiny hook he had not been able to shake loose. "Porterfield said that Archie hadn't told the whole story about the murders."

"Did he give you any idea of what the 'whole story' was?" I asked.

Doc Poole shook his head. "He just felt that Archie was covering up for somebody." He looked at me solemnly, like someone giving a dreadful diagnosis. "That somebody else was involved in the murders. Somebody besides Archie. He didn't say who he thought it was. Just somebody else."

"Why did he think that?"

"Sheriff Porterfield doesn't give reasons for what he thinks if he doesn't want to. Did Archie ever talk to you, Roy? About that night?"

"Not really," I said, still holding my brother's frantic whisper close inside: *I won't tell nobody, Roy. Nobody will ever know.*

"So, Sheriff Porterfield never brought it up to you, this idea of someone else being involved in the killings?"

"No," I said, remembering the times I'd run across Sheriff Porterfield in the days following the murders, the way he'd regarded me with a sense of catlike pursuit, waiting for me to make a wrong move.

"I guess he didn't think he needed to," Doc Poole said. "Since he knew you were with Lila."

"Did he tell you that I was with Lila at the time of the murders?"

Doc Poole tensed slightly. "Lila told him you were with her. When he went up to Waylord and talked to her. She never told you that?"

"No."

"Well, Sheriff Porterfield told me that he took Lila in for questioning and that she put him straight about the whole thing. Told him that you were with her when Archie did it."

"But he never took *me* in for questioning," I insisted. "Why would he have taken Lila's word for it?"

"I guess he believed her," Doc Poole said.

"But if Porterfield didn't believe Archie's confession, if he believed someone else had been with him that night, then why wouldn't he have at least questioned me about it?"

"I don't know, Roy. I only know that he went up to Waylord the very next morning."

I'd already gone to work at Clark's Drugs on the morning after the murders, thinking that Archie had probably made it to Nashville by then, that he and Gloria were no doubt holed up in some small hotel or rooming house, safely away from Kingdom County, never even remotely imagining that Archie hadn't fled from County Road, but had simply sat behind the wheel of his car, stunned and baffled, until Sheriff Porterfield had arrived, arrested him, and taken him to jail.

"Porterfield knew I worked at the drugstore just down the block from his office," I said. "He could have come by, asked me anything. Even taken me in for questioning like he did Lila."

"Yes, he could have."

"But he went up to Waylord instead."

"That's right," Doc Poole said. "And he never bothered talking to you because Lila told him that you were with her, and so you couldn't have had anything to do with the murders. I didn't mean to stir this whole thing up again, Roy. It was just this business of Sheriff Porterfield saying that Archie hadn't done it alone has always bothered me. But the sheriff couldn't have thought you had anything to do with it, if that's what you're thinking, Roy. Not after talking to Lila." He offered the placebo of a smile. "So, there's really no mystery, is there?"

"No," I answered, although I knew that at least one mystery remained: for if Lila had told Sheriff Porterfield I was with her at the time of the murders, she'd lied.

Why?

My father was sitting in his bed, shirtless, his back pressed up against the headboard, his gaze fixed on the flickering television screen.

"Doc Poole says you don't want any more visits," I said as I walked into the room.

"That's right."

"And no more medicine either."

He nodded, his attention still riveted to the television. "That's right. It wouldn't be fair to them bugs."

With that, he fell silent, pretending to be entirely engaged in a rerun of *I Love Lucy*, though I could tell that something was playing in his mind.

I lowered myself into the chair beside his bed. "Doc Poole mentioned something about the murders. He said Sheriff Porterfield believed that Archie didn't tell the whole story about what happened that night. Did you ever doubt that Archie told the whole story, Dad?"

"No," my father answered. He shifted about, one hand scratching at the other. "Because of the way he done it. I mean, to Horace Kellogg."

I knew what he meant. The Kelloggs had been shot repeatedly. Even so, it had never struck me that the manner of the shooting could have served as evidence against my brother, though at that moment I realized that it had done precisely that in my father's mind.

"It reminded me of Scooter," my father added. "What Archie done to Horace Kellogg. Blowing off parts of him one at a time. Figured he must have been mighty mad at him. 'Cause of the way he was treating that daughter of his. Calling her dirty names." He paused a moment, then spit out a final line, his words laced with ire. "Hitting her."

Like Henry Warren hit Deidre, I thought.

"Archie told you that?" I asked.

"Told me that night," my father said. "Said he was going to rescue Horace Kellogg's daughter. Next thing I seen, he was heading out to his car, buttoning that old checkered jacket of his."

"Rescue her," I repeated, remembering how lost and frightened Archie had looked when I'd come upon him later that same night.

"Figured he might do it too," my father said. "Just run off with that girl and them two make a life somewhere Horace Kellogg couldn't get a hold of them."

I shook my head. "They could never have done that."

"No, probably not," my father said with a sigh. "Not with Horace Kellogg in the picture. Gun-thug that he was."

"Gun-thug? Horace Kellogg was a banker, Dad."

"He was a gun-thug before that. And gun-thugs don't never change. Ain't but one thing they understand."

A terrible possibility crossed my mind. "Did you tell Archie to take a gun with him to the Kelloggs' that night?"

My father looked at me sternly. "I didn't tell Archie nothing."

"So he just took it? That old thirty-eight of yours. He just took it on his own?"

"Archie never done nothing on his own. I figured it must have been Horace Kellogg's daughter that told him to bring a gun with him."

In my mind I saw Gloria standing beside my brother as they had at Potter's store that night, snow falling in a white veil all around them, an icy wind ripping at her hair, her eyes frantic, desperate, her small hands jerking at my brother's checkered jacket.

We sat in silence for a long time, my mind replaying all I'd never been able to forget about that distant, murderous night, all the questions Porterfield might have asked: *Did you see Archie that night? What did he say to you? What did you say to him? What did he want you to do? Did you do it?*

"Sheriff Porterfield did some asking around," I said finally. "Because he didn't believe Archie's confession."

My father gave a little snort. "I ain't interested in nothing Wallace Porterfield ever done."

"Evidently he thought someone else must have been involved in the murders."

My father returned his gaze to the television. "Sounds like Porterfield was just playing with people," my father said.

"Messing with their minds."

"Did he ever speak to you?"

"No."

"He spoke to Lila. Doc Poole told me that. He said he went up to Waylord the morning after the murders and took Lila in for questioning."

My father's gaze swept back to me. "And Lila never said nothing to you about it?"

"No, never," I said. "And Porterfield never talked to me at all."

A dark fire lit my father's eyes. "He was after you though, Roy," he said with a sudden terrible certainty. "That's why he talked to Lila. 'Cause he was wanting to put them murders on you too."

I saw Archie's car beside the hedge that bordered the Kellogg house, his face peering at mine, his voice pleading, *Will you go with me, Roy?*

"There's no evidence that he was trying to pin anything on me, Dad," I said, now wanting merely to close a subject that had abruptly turned down a forbidden corner.

"No? Then how come he drove all the way up to Waylord and talked to Lila? He sure didn't think she had nothing to do with killing nobody. It must have been you he was after. It don't make you mad, him doing that?"

"After all these years? No, it doesn't make me mad."

"So you ain't gonna do nothing about it?"

"What difference would any of that make now?"

"You ain't gonna do nothing?"

"No."

He stared at me a moment, then said, "Suit yourself," and returned his eyes to the television.

Suit yourself.

Those had always been the words he'd used when he'd had enough of me.

I'm going to stay in California.

Suit yourself.

Never marry.

Suit yourself.

No kids.

Suit yourself.

"It's all too far back, Dad. It wouldn't make any difference what I found out."

My father held his gaze on the television, his eyes yellow and watery. "Suit yourself."

With that, he grasped the ball bat beside his bed, brought himself to his feet, and trudged into the bathroom, leaving me alone beside his cluttered bed.

I waited for him to return, but he never did, so after a time I rose and headed for my room. On the way I saw him in the kitchen, standing beside the refrigerator, gently holding the jar of bugs as if he preferred their company to mine.

CHAPTER SIXTEEN

Most of us make them suddenly, our most fateful choices, but those who stop to think things through rarely make any better ones. All that night, as I tossed on my bed, I reasoned that there was no point in "getting mad," no point in finding out why, twenty years before, Wallace Porterfield had thought or done anything, and certainly no reason to believe that whatever he'd thought or done could possibly matter to me now. Surely, the best argument was to let sleeping dogs lie.

But there are certain questions that we avoid at our peril, certain things that if we do not know them will forever hold our lives in thrall. That's why adopted children so often leave those who kept them to search for those who let them go. It's easy to live without knowing the history of the universe, but hard to live without knowing the history of yourself.

"Hey, Roy," Lonnie said with a wide smile when I entered his office the next morning. "You looking for another case to work on, or is this just a social call?"

"Well, actually, I *am* looking into another case."

"Oh yeah, which one?"

"Archie's," I said. "I'd like to take a look at whatever file you have on his case."

"You mean the murders?" Lonnie asked unbelievingly. "That file's nearly twenty years old, Roy. You got a reason for wanting to see it?"

"Yes, I do," I told him. "Something Doc Poole mentioned when he looked in on my father last night."

Lonnie gave a chuckle. "What would Doc Poole know about that case?"

"Well, it was actually something your father told him," I answered. "That he believed that Archie hadn't told the truth about the murders."

Lonnie offered a quick laugh. "Roy, you know as well as I do that Archie sat right in this office and told my daddy the whole story."

Standing before Lonnie's desk, looking into his eyes, I knew how frightened my brother must have been as he'd faced the far more menacing figure of Wallace Porterfield. He'd been a teenage boy from a family of no standing, easily confused, easily led, charged with the murder of a banker and his wife. How small and helpless he must have felt, something Wallace Porterfield could scrape from the bottom of his glossy boots and be done with.

"A story maybe," I told Porterfield's son. "But evidently not one your father wholeheartedly believed."

"Of course Daddy believed it," Lonnie said emphatically. "He was probably just trying to get old Doc Poole's goat."

"Well, he succeeded at that," I said dryly.

Lonnie leaned forward. "Archie confessed to the whole thing. And he never denied it. Those are the facts."

"Then why didn't your father accept them? Why did he go up to Waylord and talk to Lila Cutler?"

That Wallace Porterfield had done precisely that did not appear to surprise his only son. "A lawman has to look into lots of things, Roy. Especially in a murder case."

When I gave no response to this, Lonnie added, "You know, Roy, I've never put a man in jail that really, deep down, thought he deserved to be there. Thieves caught red-handed. Rapists. In their own minds they're always innocent. Somehow they screw it all around in their heads, and lo and behold, they come up clean. It's the way they think, criminals. The thing about Archie is that he wasn't a criminal. He just got caught up in something. Girls and all. Running off. But he wasn't a criminal. Didn't think like a criminal. When he got caught, he owned up to what he'd done. Not like a criminal, denying everything no matter how much evidence you

185

have. Archie told the truth flat out."

When I continued to stare at Lonnie silently, his voice turned grave. "You're set on this, aren't you?"

"Yes, I am."

He chuckled dryly. "Okay, Roy," he said. "I'll see that you get that file."

I waited.

"I don't mean right now." Lonnie eased himself back in his chair. "Those files are over at my daddy's house. He keeps them in his garage."

"Those are county files, Lonnie. They don't belong to your father."

" 'Course not," Lonnie said. "He's just storing them, that's all."

"Well, I'd like to see the file on Archie as soon as possible."

He heard the threat in my voice, the fact that if I didn't get access to Archie's file right away, I might just make a call to the state capital, raise the legal issue of why official state records were currently being stored on the property of a man who no longer had authority over them.

"Okay, Roy, if you're sure."

I had never been more sure of anything in my life.

Wallace Porterfield came out of his house as I brought my car to a halt beside the shimmering black Lincoln that sat luxuriously in his driveway. He was dressed in black pants and a white short-sleeve shirt, and he descended the stairs with surprising speed, still powerful in his old age, with muscular arms and legs, a charging bull of a man.

"Lonnie says you want to see that file on the Kellogg murders," he said.

"That's right."

He came toward me with the wide, striding gait I remembered from the night he'd led me from Archie's cell for the last time, both of us passing Doc Poole on the way.

Once we'd gone through the thick door that separated the sheriff's office from the short block of cells, he'd stepped aside to let me by, saying only that I was a "lucky boy." In what way, I wondered now, had Porterfield thought me lucky?

"That file's stuck in with a lot of other stuff." He waved me forward, his gigantic hand floating like a huge brown raptor in the summer air. "This way."

I followed him across the lawn much as I'd followed him out of my brother's cell and down the long corridor to the office all those years before. Of all the men I'd ever seen, he appeared the least weakened by his great age, not at all the withered scarecrow my father had become.

At the garage he bent forward and drew up the door.

"The stuff's not in any particular order,"

he warned as he stepped into its darkened interior. "You'll just have to go through it."

He yanked a string. A naked lightbulb revealed a wall of cardboard boxes, each with a date scrawled in black ink.

"You can narrow it down by the year, at least," Porterfield told me. "It's all sorted by the year." He squinted at the boxes. "It was about twenty years ago, wasn't it? When your brother killed 'em?" His ancient eyes drifted toward me. "And you went off to college about that same time."

"Just a week or so later," I answered, remembering Porterfield's words, struck by how true they'd been, the fact that the old sheriff really did know everything, the dark recesses of his kingdom.

Porterfield's eyes swept back into the shadowy interior of the garage. "Well, there they are, the records. How long will you need? An hour, something like that?"

"It shouldn't take long, once I find the file."

I expected him to turn, go back to the house, but instead he continued to stand before me, his great head slumped forward, the dark eyes bearing down upon me.

"Lonnie said old Doc Poole set your bowels to blubbering," he said. "Got you all shook up about things."

"Not exactly shook up. He just mentioned that you didn't buy Archie's story."

"Well, I guess I should have just kept my big mouth shut, then," Sheriff Porterfield said with a grim smile. "Especially knowing what a big mouth Doc Poole's got. He's sort of a gossip, you know. Talking through his hat all the time. Believes anything he's told. Lucky he was born with a dick instead of a pussy, or he'd have been knocked up all the time." He laughed, then sucked his laughter back in when he saw that I hadn't joined him in it. "You came by the jail that last night. Walked you out, I remember that."

"You have a powerful memory, Sheriff."

"Fair enough."

"The night Archie died, you said I was lucky. As I was leaving your office. That I was lucky."

Porterfield stared at me, his face unreadable as a granite slab.

"In what way did you think I was lucky, Sheriff?"

"That you'd stayed out of trouble, I guess," he said. "Not like that brother of yours."

But the true answer flickered instantly in his eyes, so that I knew the one he gave me was a lie.

"She was above him, but he didn't pay that any mind. That's what fucked him up." Once again the dark eyes tried to squeeze me into something small. "You had more sense. Stayed with your kind. That girl in Waylord. Lila Cutler. The one you was dating back

189

then. Fact is, your brother should have taken a page from your book. Dipped his pen in some Waylord girl, not in Horace Kellogg's daughter."

"How do you know I dipped my pen in anybody?"

His dry chuckle rattled between us. "Anybody dates a Waylord girl's bound to get a little."

"They're never fresh, you mean." I said it coldly.

Rather than answer, Porterfield said, "Problem is, that brother of yours got stuck on a valley girl." Again his laughter jangled. "Got himself all fucked up over a girl that wasn't even that pretty. Not like that one of yours."

Then I knew what Porterfield had meant about my being lucky. It was that I'd been lucky to have Lila Cutler, known the pleasure of a body that must have seemed to him, in the grim throes of middle age, impossibly sweet and young.

"You talked to Lila. The day after the murders," I said.

Something moved behind his eyes, silent as a shadow.

"Why didn't you ever talk to me?" I asked.

He shrugged indifferently, neither curious about nor alarmed by the question.

"Was it because Lila cleared me?" I asked. "Told you that I was with her at the time of the murders?"

"It wouldn't have mattered to me what that girl said. Where you was. I wouldn't of cared."

"But you told Doc Poole that you thought someone else was involved in the murders."

"Doc Poole again." There was a cold edge in the old man's voice. "That old bastard ought to keep his pie-hole shut."

"Did you tell him that?"

"Sure did. Still believe it too."

"Then why didn't you ever question me about it?"

He released a small, sneering chuckle. "Because a man has to have some fight in him to kill two people. Some gumption." A smile slithered onto his lips. "And the way I heard it, you didn't even fight back when that pretty little girlfriend of yours got insulted."

His son's voice pierced the air, *Waylord girls ain't never fresh.*

"But you thought that Archie had the 'gumption' for it?"

Porterfield peered at me as if, using his eyes alone, he could burn holes in my soul. "I'm sure that somebody came along with him that night," he answered. "Went into the house with him too. Maybe even did the shooting. There was two sets of footprints in the snow. It was melting fast, that snow, 'cause the sun was up and it was getting mighty warm. But I saw them just the same. One set of footprints went back and forth from the driver's side of your brother's car to the house. But the other one went back and forth from the passenger side of that car. So somebody was in the car with your brother, and got out of that car, and walked up to that house with him. And that somebody come back and set with him, I guess, in that car."

"So where was this second person when you arrested Archie?"

He smiled. "Just take a look at that stuff you're wanting to see so much. Everything's there. Everything that had anything to do with the murders. Even that gun your brother did it with." He looked at me pointedly. "You'd recognize it, wouldn't you? That old thirty-eight? Found it on the seat right next to your brother. Figured he was thinking about putting an end to himself right there. There was one bullet left, you know. Figured he'd saved it for himself. But he found another way, didn't he?"

In my mind I saw my brother hanging from the black bars, the jailhouse bedsheet twisted into a noose. I stayed silent.

"Take a good long look in that file," Porterfield said. "At that old gun too." There was a grim challenge in his voice, like someone coaxing a child to open a box where, as he already knew, a viper lay coiled. "Take a real close look at all that stuff."

"I intend to," I said stiffly.

Porterfield smiled but said nothing else. Instead, he turned and headed back toward the house, his tread heavy with age and dreadful experience, moving like an old mastodon toward his granite cave, still so huge he seemed almost to shake the earth as he moved away.

CHAPTER SEVENTEEN

I found the file on the murders a few minutes later, a file so slender it could be contained in a single nine-by-twelve envelope, the word KELLOGG scrawled in smudged ink in the left corner. Porterfield's initial report lay inside, along with Archie's confession and Gloria's statement.

The first thing I noticed as I read through the file was that there'd been no call summoning Wallace Porterfield to the Kellogg house that night. He'd simply descended upon it from out of the snowy darkness.

The time was 5:14 a.m., a very strange time indeed for the sheriff to have seen what he claimed he saw as he made his early-morning rounds, first patrolling back and forth along the deserted, snowbound streets of Kingdom City before extending his vigilance northward, along County Road.

As he'd neared the mailbox at the end of the driveway at 1411, his statement said, he'd noticed an old Ford parked beside the tall hedge that bordered the grounds of Horace Kellogg's home.

The house itself was ablaze with lights so that it shone out of the blackness, a circumstance Porterfield found suspicious given the hour and his longtime familiarity with the routine of his old friend; the fact, as he carefully noted in his report, was that Horace and Lavenia Kellogg were both "early-to-bed types."

Even so, it was less the lighted house that attracted Porterfield's attention than the car he saw parked beside the hedge.

And so he'd pulled up behind the Ford rather than turning into the Kelloggs' driveway. Getting out of his cruiser, he'd peered at a figure who sat motionless behind the wheel in the car's unlighted interior.

According to Porterfield's report, Archie made no attempt to conceal what had happened inside Horace Kellogg's house moments before. Instead, he'd straightened himself abruptly when Porterfield neared him, like a frightened little boy before a demanding teacher, and said in a broken voice I could easily imagine, "Didn't mean to, Sheriff. Didn't mean for it to happen."

Porterfield had scrawled only a few sketchy notes about the conversation he'd had with my brother during the next few seconds, but it was not hard for me to reconstruct the old sheriff's authoritative questions, nor Archie's fearful responses:

What are you taking about, son?
So fast.

You're Archie Slater, right. Been dating Horace's girl?

In there. They're in there.

"In there" Sheriff Porterfield had found first Lavenia Kellogg sprawled at the bottom of the stairs, facedown, one arm still clawing upward, hand on the second step, her legs spread apart, her shattered eyeglasses resting between them.

As any other lawman would have done, Wallace Porterfield immediately abandoned any further search of the house, rushed back down the snow-covered drive to where Archie still waited behind the wheel of his car, and confronted him with what he'd just found.

Did you do this, boy?

Didn't mean for her to see it.

Wallace Porterfield had needed nothing more but had instantly handcuffed Archie to the steering wheel of his car, then fired his next question:

Is Gloria dead too?

No.

How about Horace?

I didn't mean for her to see it.

He'd found Gloria in her upstairs bedroom, curled like a fetus in the womb within the

196

covers of her bed, sobbing, utterly inco-
herent, so that Porterfield had made no attempt to question her, but had called Doc
Poole instead, then returned downstairs.
There he found Horace Kellogg crouched in
a corner of his den, his back pressed up
against its wood-paneled wall, body bent forward, his hair touching the blood-soaked
carpet beneath his shattered head.

A cheap thirty-eight with a brown wooden
handle lay a few feet from Horace. Porterfield returned to Archie and only then noticed the old gun that rested on the seat
beside him. He seized it immediately.

Is this yours, son?
I took it from my daddy.
Your daddy? Jesse Slater?
Yes, sir.

In my mind I could see the old sheriff
turn, notice for the first time the physical detail he'd later described in his report, that
there was a second set of tracks in the snow
which led from the Ford to the Kellogg
house, then back down to the car. They
could not have been Archie's — they
emerged from the passenger side of the
truck, then wound upward, through the
snowdrifts to the front door of the house.

Someone else, I thought, the very knowledge
that must have sounded in Porterfield's mind

at that moment convinced him in an instant that Archie had brought someone with him, someone who'd helped him murder Horace and Lavenia Kellogg.

The interrogation that followed was hardly surprising:

Who else was involved in this, son?
Nobody.
You sure?
Yes, sir.
You shot Horace Kellogg?
Yes, sir, I did.
Just you?
Nobody else had nothing to do with it.
So you killed them both?
So fast.

He'd taken Archie to jail in Kingdom City, then, according to his report, returned to the Kellogg house to find Gloria sedated, sleeping deeply, Doc Poole in a chair beside her bed. He'd left the two as he'd found them, then gone downstairs and examined the bodies.

It was at that point he'd noticed Horace Kellogg's other wounds, one in the arm, one in the knee, a finger on the right hand blown away, the lobe of the left ear shot off, a bloodstained hole in his blue shirt just below the third button, all this indicating that Horace Kellogg had not only been murdered but murdered with callous cruelty, "taken out in pieces," as Porterfield had written in his report.

Two days later Doc Poole's autopsy reached the same conclusion, one that fit perfectly with the description Gloria Kellogg had, by then, given of her parents' murders, and which Sheriff Porterfield duly appended to his report.

In her statement Gloria described most of the events leading up to the killings, everything from her first meeting with Archie to their last date. She detailed the argument she'd had with her father on the night of the murders, how she'd fled the house, and found her way to Potter's store. She'd called Archie from there, a call that had been "picked up," as she put it, by my father, who'd handed the phone over to Archie.

She'd waited at Potter's store until Archie arrived, along with Lila and me. The four of us had gone to the movies in Kingdom City, then she'd been dropped off once again at Potter's. In the frigid darkness of that country store, Gloria said, Archie had declared that he would come and get her at first light. He would honk his horn once as he approached the house, then turn off the headlights and drift the rest of the way, coming to a halt behind the wall of shrubs that stood at the driveway.

At just after five a.m. she'd heard the horn

and slipped to the window of her upstairs room. From there she'd seen the roof of Archie's car behind the hedge. She'd hastily finished packing the suitcase for the elopement and headed for the door.

Before she'd reached it she heard the doorbell, then her mother say "Dear God," then a shot. This was followed by other shots, shots that had frozen her in place, stunned and mute, until the last echo died away.

She had no idea what Archie had done after that, she claimed, though she believed he must have remained in the house for a time. Finally she'd heard the front door open and assumed that he'd left, headed for his car, as she supposed, although she'd never heard it pull away.

For good reason, since the old Ford had still been parked beside the hedge at 5:14, when Sheriff Porterfield pulled up behind it, and found Archie.

I turned to the photographs Porterfield included in the file. Looking at them, I couldn't imagine such capacity for destruction in my brother's makeup, could not fit my brother's fingers around the wooden handle of the pistol Porterfield had found, and which, without doubt, had been brought with him from my father's house.

For a long time I stared down at the pictures, Lavenia Kellogg's blasted head, the tortured body of her husband, and struggled to picture my brother holding the gun that had carried out these murders, reaching for it in his belt, squeezing down on the trigger, watching as small geysers of blood leapt from the fleeing bodies, splattering walls, pooling on the floor. In the midst of all this horror, Archie remained utterly incongruous, a piece I could not make fit in a murderous puzzle.

Other pieces fit perfectly, however. A white identification tag hung from the trigger guard of my father's gun, but otherwise it was the same thirty-eight my father had handed to Archie as we'd crossed the field toward Scooter. It still contained the single shell Porterfield had mentioned earlier, the old sheriff so supremely confident that he alone would retain possession of my father's gun that he had not even bothered to unload the murder weapon.

Holding it now, feeling its weight, its terrible reality, I still could not imagine Archie aiming it at anyone. And yet, he had incontestably confessed to two murders, admitted them immediately, in his first conversation, if it could be called that, with Porterfield. Nor over the next three days had he recanted a single word of that confession despite the many opportunities he'd had to do so. Times when I'd been alone with him in his cell, when he could have merely leaned over, whispered, *I didn't do it,* and left the rest to me.

In fact, rather than take back a single word of what he'd said to Porterfield outside the Kellogg house, Archie had consistently elaborated upon the events he'd only haltingly described on that first occasion, adding more and more detail, painting an utterly persuasive picture of how he'd drawn up behind the hedge, honked to signal Gloria, then, when she did not emerge, trudged up the snowy drive to the house.

He'd encountered Mrs. Kellogg at the door, he said. She'd told him that Gloria was upstairs in her room, and that the girl was going to stay there. She'd tried to close the door in my brother's face, but Archie said he'd pushed it back open and stepped inside. Mrs. Kellogg had then called for her husband, he said, an act that had panicked him so that he'd reached beneath his hunting jacket to where my father's pistol was tucked inside his belt.

Mrs. Kellogg had screamed, Archie said, then turned toward the stairs. That's when he'd fired. One shot. Directly into the back of Lavenia Kellogg's skull. She'd fallen backward, then tumbled down the stairs, landing at their foot just as Horace entered from the adjoining living room. Like his wife, he'd fled at the sight of the gun in Archie's hand, back toward the rear of the house, Archie following him all the way, firing as he went, hitting Mr. Kellogg again and again, until they'd finally reached the den. Kellogg had rushed for the gun cabinet, his wounded leg buckling under him, so that he'd finally stumbled into the corner beside the cabinet, the spot where Archie had at last caught up with him and fired the shot that killed him. After that, Archie had run back through the living room to the front door and then out of the house and down the path to the old Ford, where he remained, waiting for Gloria, everything a blur until a light flashed in the distance, two headlights coming toward him, snow sparkling in their narrow beams.

This was the story my brother told and re-told, and it was easy for me to imagine him sitting in his stark cell, Porterfield standing near its center, crowding the cramped space, drawing in the light.

And yet Porterfield's intimidating presence had failed to elicit from my brother the one thing the old sheriff had already come to suspect: that someone else had been with him that night, either egging him on to murder, or committing murder himself.

I had no doubt that Porterfield had spent a great deal of time talking to Archie, for the final confession had to have been pieced together by Porterfield himself. Archie, in the best of times, would not have been able to accomplish such a fluid narrative. And yet, for all the many times Porterfield had coaxed Archie to tell it one more time, my brother had persistently refused to reveal at least one detail of that bloody night, the fact that I'd stopped on the road across from his car, rolled down my window, and called to him.

Hey, Arch, what are you doing?
We're running off, Roy. Gloria and me.
You mean, right now?
Right now.
Where you going?
Nashville, I guess.
So, you're really going to do it?
Yeah. I got to, I guess.

I might have stopped him, I thought now, might have gotten out of my car, walked over to my brother, and brought the whole foolish scheme to a grinding halt. I knew it would have taken no more than a few words from me to have changed his mind, nothing more than the most rudimentary reminder that he had little money and no job, that he knew no one in Nashville who might lend them a helping hand. Hadn't he even given me the perfect opportunity to do all of that?

But I'd left him there, waiting for Gloria, as I pulled away, the feel of Lila's body still warm on mine, mindlessly joyful with what I'd proven to myself only minutes before, that Lila Cutler was indeed "fresh," a wild happiness flooding through me, blinding me to my

204

brother's peril so that I'd offered him nothing but a wink and some careless words of advice that he'd never mentioned to Wallace Porterfield, words I'd said only minutes before the murders, my final words, as it had turned out, before leaving my brother to his fate: *Okay, Arch, but don't leave any witnesses.*

CHAPTER EIGHTEEN

"You 'bout finished up in there?"

I turned toward the door of the garage, the old pistol still in my hand, and peered out to where Wallace Porterfield stood like a stone, blocking the light. His eyes fell toward the pistol. "Just throw that thing back in the box," he said, now clearly impatient to be done with me.

I turned back toward the box, intending to return the pistol to it, then I felt an irrational need to defy Wallace Porterfield, and instead tucked the old gun into my belt and covered it with my shirt.

"Hurry up, now," Porterfield said. "I got business to attend to."

I paid no heed, but methodically returned the files to the envelope, then the envelope to the box.

"Don't play with me, boy. Don't ever do that."

Before I could respond, he snorted. "You don't favor your daddy. He was a pretty good-looking kid." He smiled. "I taught him a lesson once." His eyes were two dark fires. "Saved him from a world of trouble. Fucking shame he didn't teach the same lesson to your brother."

I said it coldly: "To know his place."

The smile vanished, and Porterfield stared at me now, like a hawk watching a small gray mouse scurry across an exposed field. "So you know about that lesson I gave your daddy? I figured he must have told you about it."

"He never told me, no," I answered. "I heard about it in Waylord."

Porterfield seemed pleased that the tale was still being recounted. Then another thought appeared to enter his mind, crowding all thought of my father and that lesson in brutality entirely from his brain. "Find anything in that file you wanted to look at?"

"As a matter of fact, I did."

He caught the steely tone in my voice, but it meant nothing to him, all bravado the same, equally empty, all men the same, but half of him.

"What's that?"

"I noticed you've got Archie's statement and Gloria's, but one statement's missing. The one you took from Lila Cutler."

"Why would I have a statement from her?"

"Because you took her in for questioning. So I was just wondering where her statement is."

"I probably didn't write one up," Porterfield answered, sounding weary of being confronted with such a tedious and inconsequential matter.

Even so, I pressed him. "Which would have been unusual for you."

His eyes turned cold. "You got any other questions, son?"

"Well, actually, I do. I was wondering where that second person went. The one who came with Archie. You never told me who you thought it was."

"There's no way of knowing that," Porterfield answered.

"But you must have a theory?"

"My theory is that whoever came with your brother that night didn't want to get caught the way your brother did. And so this second person up and left."

"Left for where?"

"Well, let me see," Porterfield said, broadly pretending to speculate on the matter. "Left for home, I guess. Left for wherever he'd come from. Through the woods maybe. That's where you live, right? Over around Cantwell?"

"Yes."

"That's less than a mile from the Kellogg house as the crow flies, wouldn't you say?"

"Probably."

"So this second person could have gone on foot. Whoever it was that came with your brother in that old car of his could have gone right through the woods, and there wouldn't have been no sign of it. Snow would have covered his tracks by full daylight."

"So I guess you'll never know who it was," I told him.

"I guess not," he said, growing impatient again. "Come on out of there now, I got things to do."

I stepped out of the garage, watched as he closed and locked the door.

"I still have a few questions," I said. "About the investigation."

He seemed barely to hear me, or to care so little about what I'd said that he felt no need to respond.

"About what Archie told you when you talked to him."

Porterfield lumbered back toward his house, throwing words over his shoulder. "Who cares what that boy told me? It wasn't the truth anyway. Except in patches." He stopped, turned, and looked me dead in the eye. "He left things out, you know. Said he didn't see a living soul after he got to the house that night." He waited for me to respond, or perhaps only to squirm beneath his accusatory gaze. "But he saw you, didn't he, Roy?"

"Yes, he did."

As if satisfied with my answer, Porterfield turned and headed toward his car, his great bulk casting a black stain over the ground beside him. "Saw you, but didn't tell me a thing about it."

"I pulled up just across the road from

him," I said, walking quickly in order to keep at his side.

"I know you did." Porterfield's eyes were on the Lincoln now, staring at it intently, as if looking for a smudge on its shiny exterior.

"And if you'd ever asked me about it, I'd have told you so."

"Maybe you would have. But your brother didn't. That's the point."

"He was trying to protect me. Trying to make sure I didn't get . . . that I wouldn't be a suspect."

"I knew he was protecting somebody," Porterfield said. "Knew all the time that he wasn't dealing with me straight."

We reached his car.

Porterfield grabbed the door handle but didn't open it.

"But there wasn't any need to press him on it," he told me. "Because I already knew that you never got out of your car. So whether you were there or not, it didn't matter to me as far as those killings were concerned. You never got out of your car. End of story."

"How do you know I never got out of my car?" I persisted.

" 'Cause I got spies everywhere, son," Porterfield said as he jerked the handle and yanked open the car door. "I got eyes in the clouds. Step back now, I got to go." He began to roll up the window.

Eyes in the clouds, I thought, watching him drop into his big black Lincoln, half believing that he did possess such vast malignant powers.

"How did you know I didn't get out of my car that night?" I asked.

"What difference does it make, long as I knew it wasn't you that came with your brother over to Horace Kellogg's house. Who it was that did come with him, that's what I wanted to know. But he never broke on that, your brother. Never told me who it was." He began to roll up the window. "Step back, now, I got to go."

I put my hand on the glass. "You think it was my father."

The window stopped its upward glide, but Porterfield didn't answer, and in that interval I saw Archie lean toward the passenger door of the old Ford rather than scoot over to it, lean far over whatever blocked his way, something in the front seat, I imagined suddenly, hunched down, hidden.

"Son, is that something you really want to know?" An unmistakable hint of warning crawled into Porterfield's voice, a sense of someone who already knew what lay in wait behind the unopened door.

"Of course it is."

"Well, why don't you figure it out for yourself, then. You like playing cop, don't you? Figure it out. It's not that hard."

"Why don't you just tell me," I demanded.

Porterfield's eyes glowed. "Whose gun was it? The one I found next to your brother?"

I saw the pistol pass from my father's hand to Archie's on the morning he'd forced him to kill Scooter, felt something deep inside myself first shudder, then grow cold. "It was my father's gun," I said.

"Yep, it was," Porterfield agreed quietly. "And his fingerprints were probably all over it. But what would that prove? It was his gun, 'course it would have his fingerprints on it. But you don't just get evidence from guns and such. They's always a man that's part of it, that has to go with it."

I could see something curling around in Porterfield's mind, a small black snake.

"So I asked myself," he added, "who would have had the gumption to do such a thing? And a reason to do it? A reason to get back at Horace, shoot him the way he was shot. Who would have hated Horace that much?"

I stared at him, puzzled.

"Your daddy never told you about Horace?"

"He said he was a gun-thug."

"He was a deputy is what he was," Porterfield said. "Worked for me as a deputy for quite a few years. Came with me up to Waylord when I had business there. People to straighten out. People that had got above themselves. People that needed to be taught a lesson. People like your daddy."

I saw the dark men who'd closed in on my father by the candy counter of the Waylord company store.

"Kellogg helped you," I said. "With that . . . lesson?"

Porterfield grinned. "He wasn't much older than your daddy was, but Horace sure did his share."

The one thing I would not let myself do at that moment was collapse under the great weight of what Porterfield had just revealed.

"But you never even talked to my father," I said. "You never even questioned him about whether he was —"

"Why should I?" Porterfield blurted out. He regarded me as if I were a small child stupidly fending off an enormous dragon. "Jesse Slater wouldn't have said anything to me. Not like that whining brother of yours. Sputtering and crying. Jesse wouldn't have broken down like that. Never. Got too much gumption." He shrugged. "I figured that in the end, I'd get it out of your brother, but once he was dead there was nothing I could do but drop the whole thing, just let your daddy go. Pride, that was your daddy's downfall. Too much pride for a little shit Waylord boy." He cackled dryly. "But like I said, I knew it couldn't have been you shooting that gun. Because you don't have your daddy's gumption."

He hit the button inside the car and turned toward the wheel as the darkly tinted window glided into place.

During the next few minutes I learned just how swiftly and completely denial can block the mind's communication with the heart. For as I watched Porterfield back out of the driveway of his house, my own mind furiously blocked me from any serious consideration of the terrible suspicion the old sheriff had voiced about my father.

And so, during the next few seconds I went over everything about that murderous night but the possibility that my father could have had anything to do with it.

Methodically, meticulously, I relived every detail of it again, so that I saw myself behind the wheel of the Chevy, heading up to Waylord at just before six that evening, gray clouds already hanging low and dark overhead, feeling again the cold drizzle they released as I came to a halt in Lila's drive.

Lila had come out immediately, dashing happily across the bare yard, wrapped in a dark red coat, a clear plastic rain hat around her hair. Bursts of mist came from her mouth as she leapt into my car, snuggling up against me, smiling, pretending to shiver, *Brrrr.*

We'd headed back down to the valley, talking all the way, full of the brilliant future we'd begun to imagine for ourselves, that I'd go to college, get my degree, then return and marry her. I'd get a teaching job and then she'd go to college too. We'd raise a family. The future had never looked brighter than on that snowy night.

The more immediate plan was far more achievable, of course: a double date no different from the many others we'd had in the past.

Archie was pacing back and forth when Lila and I pulled into the driveway that evening. He looked stricken and confused, the way he always did when things began to overwhelm him.

"We can't pick up Gloria at her house," he said as he threw himself into the backseat of my car. "She had a big fight with her daddy and ran over to Potter's Grocery."

The first scattered flakes of snow began to fall as we pulled up to Potter's Grocery. Gloria was waiting anxiously behind its misty front window, her expression hardly less stricken than Archie's.

Her tone was grave as she slid into the backseat. "I don't know what Daddy's going to do, Archie."

Archie drew her beneath his arm. "Maybe we'll just run off, then," he said.

We decided to go to the movie house in Kingdom City. Once there, Gloria and Archie went directly to the counter to buy popcorn, leaving Lila and me at the front of the theater.

"He'll do it, you know," Lila told me. "He'll run off with Gloria."

"They wouldn't get very far, Lila."

"That doesn't matter," Lila said darkly. "Gloria's underage. Her father could call the sheriff and have him arrested."

I glanced over to the concession stand, watched as Archie paid for a bag of popcorn, then handed it to Gloria.

"He wouldn't try to take Gloria away," I told Lila confidently. "Even if he wanted to, he wouldn't know how to do it."

I was still holding firmly to that conviction when the movie ended two hours later. We drove Gloria back to her house, where she and Archie stood briefly at the end of the driveway, hidden behind the hedge.

"Gloria's really upset," Archie said, when he got back in the car. "She thinks her daddy's gonna beat her up."

Lila's eyes shot back toward my brother. "Be careful, Archie, please. Be really careful."

The snow had thickened by the time we reached the house. For a moment, Archie remained in the backseat of the car as if in dread of what the night might bring were he left to his own devices.

"It's going to work out, Archie," I assured him. "We'll talk it all through when I get back."

He nodded reluctantly, and got out of the car, moved halfway up the driveway, then stopped as if by a black wall.

"Go talk to him," Lila urged me. "He's lost without you."

I did as she asked, got out of the car and walked over to my brother.

"Everything's going to work out," I promised him. "Believe me, Arch, everything's going to work out."

"What if I was to do it, Roy? We could go to —"

"Listen, just go inside and stay there." I smiled. "We'll talk it over in the morning."

Archie did not smile back. "Her daddy's hurting her real bad, the things he's saying to her. It's not right, Roy, Calling her names. Hurting her like that. Threatening her."

I placed my hand on his shoulder, a little annoyed. "Archie, do what I told you. Go inside. In the morning, we'll talk it over. There's nothing you can do tonight anyway."

He nodded slowly, heavily, in that ponderous way of his. "Okay, Roy . . ." A small, tentative smile broke over his face. "Thanks."

"Are we clear on this, then?"

"Yeah, we're clear."

"Good," I said, then glanced toward the house and saw my father standing in the lighted window. He was watching us, his eyes like two cold lights shining through the snow.

"Go on inside now," I told my brother.

"Yeah, right," Archie said, and stepped away.

I darted back to the Chevy, expecting to see Archie already lumbering up the stairs and into the house. But he was still standing only a few feet from where I'd left him, as deep in thought as was possible for him, struggling to find a way out of his confusion.

"He'll be all right," I told Lila as I turned the ignition.

Lila's eyes bored into my brother. "It won't end here," she murmured.

She had never spoken more truly, it struck me now, as I watched Wallace Porterfield's car move down the long road that fronted his house. For it never had.

CHAPTER NINETEEN

He was on the front porch when I pulled into the driveway a few minutes later, his body tilted back in a spindly chair, his bare feet pressed down upon the unpainted wooden slats, a gaunt figure I could scarcely envision as the raging, vengeful man Wallace Porterfield had conjured up.

And yet, I knew that age and illness are deceptive, that old killers must surely look like all old men, infirm and vaguely sorrowful. And so it was a younger, stronger man I made myself imagine as I studied him through the windshield, a man who'd sputtered madly as he'd loaded the pistol, his mind ablaze with what Horace Kellogg had done to him so many years before, all life suddenly reduced to a score he had to settle.

"Where you been?" he demanded as I got out of my car.

"I talked to Lonnie about what Doc Poole told me last night."

"I thought didn't none of that matter to you."

"I changed my mind."

He scowled. "You ain't gonna get no help from Lonnie."

"Well, he didn't think much of the idea of my looking into Archie's case, that's true. But he didn't try to stop me."

I came up the stairs, staring closely at my father, as if it were actually possible to look past his age and withered appearance, determine if he could have done what Wallace Porterfield suspected, murdered a man and a woman in cold blood.

"He sent me over to Wallace Porterfield's house," I added. "It seems he keeps the county police files in his garage. They don't belong to him, of course, but he keeps them anyway."

"Nobody ever made Wallace Porterfield do right," my father said, his voice swelling with rancor, so that it suddenly struck me that revenge was perhaps the real engine that had propelled his life.

"Porterfield believes that you came with Archie to Horace Kellogg's house that night," I told him bluntly.

My father snorted but gave no other response.

I sat down next to him. "He thought you might have committed the murders, then walked back here through the woods."

"Why would I have murdered them people? I didn't care nothing about Horace Kellogg's daughter."

"But you knew Kellogg, didn't you?"

"I knew him."

"According to Porterfield, there was bad blood between the two of you."

My father didn't meet my eyes. "Told you I killed him 'cause of that?"

"Well, it would have been a motive, wouldn't it?" I drew the pistol from beneath my shirt. "And it was your gun."

"Where'd you get that?"

"I took it from a box of stuff Porterfield had."

"Why'd you do that, Roy? So you could show it to me? You believe him, don't you?"

"There were tracks," I said. "Footprints. It looked like someone came with Archie to Kellogg's house that night. In his car, I mean. Walked up to the house with him."

"And you think it was me?"

"I'm just telling you what Porterfield thinks."

"I don't give a shit what Wallace Porterfield thinks. I'm asking what you think!"

When I didn't answer, he added, "What about the woman, Roy? Horace Kellogg's wife. She was killed too, ain't that right?"

"Yes."

"In all your life, Roy, have you ever seen me lift my hand against a woman?"

In all my life, I had not.

"I wasn't the best husband ever was, but did you ever see me touch your mother, no matter how mad I got?"

He peered at the gun as if it were a decaying carcass. "Don't lay no murder of a woman on me. 'Cause it ain't right to think I'd do something like that."

I realized then the vast effect of my father's lost romance, that Deidre Warren's death, the part he'd played in it, had forever placed him beyond the harming of a woman. Men he might cheerfully destroy with the single sweep of a flaming sword, but no woman would ever have a thing to fear from him.

"Porterfield was just goading you," he added now. "It's a game he's always liked. Making people believe stuff about each other that ain't so. He done it up in Waylord all the time. Played people off against each other. He liked doing it. Made him feel powerful. Bet he done it to Lila too, that time he talked to her about the murders."

"Done what?"

"Planted something in her mind," my father answered. "About you. You said it was never the same between you and Lila," he went on, and I could see the storm begin to take shape in his mind. "Never the same after them killings."

"Yes, but that had —"

"Maybe it was Porterfield caused that," my father interrupted. "Maybe Porterfield played with Lila when he went up and talked to her that day. Told her it was *you* done the killings. Put *that* in her head."

Suddenly, without my willing it, this

222

seemed entirely plausible. "He might have," I admitted. "I mean, I was there that night."

"You was there?" my father asked. His eyes were two probing needles. "You seen Archie?"

"He was just sitting in his car," I said. "Waiting to go up to the house, I guess. Still trying to figure out what to do." What I had done fell upon me like a heavy stone. "And I let him down. I'd been with Lila, and I was . . . I don't know . . . I just wasn't thinking. So I didn't try to stop him. I just wished him luck and told him . . . well . . . not to leave . . . any . . . not to leave any witnesses."

My father turned away and stared out at the deserted road.

"Archie never told Porterfield about my being there," I went on. "But Porterfield knew it anyway. He told me that this afternoon. That he'd always known I was there that night."

My father remained silent. He stared at me as if he'd never seen me before.

"No one ever knew about my being there," I said. "I never told anyone. I guess I was . . . ashamed of what I said to Archie, that I may have contributed, you know, to what he did."

My father chewed his bottom lip for a moment, then said, "Well, if Archie never told Porterfield you was there, and you never told nobody, then how come he knew it?"

"I asked him that myself. He just said he had eyes in the clouds."

My father sniffed. "Ain't nobody got eyes in the clouds. Not even Wallace Porterfield. Somebody had to have told him, Roy. Ain't no other way he could have found out about it." He seemed to be watching a strange conspiracy unfold, and was now so deep in thought, he seemed almost a different person, solemn, meditative, like one abruptly awakened to all he'd let blindly pass. "Ain't nobody else could have told Porterfield nothing about that night.

"Gloria," he murmured. "It must have been Gloria."

CHAPTER TWENTY

I started looking for her the very next morning, before my father rose. I knew that I could have once again gone to Lonnie, asked him if he had any idea of what had become of Gloria Kellogg after the murder of her parents, but by then I'd come to see him as my father did, not just as the son of Wallace Porterfield but the keeper of Porterfield's malicious flame.

And so rather than go to Lonnie's office, I went to the little redbrick building that housed the Kingdom County Library.

I started with the back issues of the *Kingdom City Banner*, the only newspaper in Kingdom County. By the extent of the coverage it became clear that the *Banner* had regarded the two killings as the major news event of the decade. Ministers had used the crime to rail against the evils of modern life, citing the movies, books, and even the drugstore detective novels they claimed my brother had habitually read, though I knew that he'd never gotten more than a few pages into any one of them before he'd passed it over to me.

I'd left Kingdom County shortly after Archie's death, and so I'd never read anything concerning the aftermath of the homicides. Because of that, I was stunned to learn how viciously my brother had been demonized in those weeks following the murders. Even his suicide in the county jail had done little to dampen the community's blazing outrage. Weeks after the murders, his name was invoked in articles and editorials, used as an example of all that was "cancerous" in American youth.

Not even Archie's teachers had found anything good to say about him. He'd "seemed sweet," they said, but this sweetness might well have been no more than the "clever ruse" of a boy who all seemed to have forgotten was by no means clever.

The brother I'd known and loved was obliterated in all of this, so much transformed that in photographs he appeared eerily sinister even to me, a boy staring dead-eyed at the camera, dull and emotionless, Sheriff Porterfield perpetually rising like a huge column at his side.

Oddly enough, it was Porterfield who'd offered the only defense of Archie, though it was no more than an official recognition that he'd never been in trouble before, nor given anyone reason to suspect him capable of such a crime. Of his suicide, Porterfield had said only, "Well, I guess God's justice was served," and left any further public comment to others.

As for Gloria Kellogg, she'd made no comment of any kind ever, as far as I could find. The papers told me no more than I'd learned at the time, that Gloria had been found upstairs in her bed, taken into custody by Sheriff Porterfield, then released after having made a statement which in every detail backed up my brother's confession.

After that, as far as the old accounts were concerned, Gloria had simply vanished, so that I had no way of knowing where she'd gone or what had happened to her, or whether, in the deep, deep night, she ever heard those shots again, felt her soul freeze behind the bedroom door.

If so, I could find no hint of it, no trail to follow, and yet I continued to sit at the library table, working with a fierce determination that was not in the least intellectual, and which would not release me until I finally chanced upon a single short news item.

It had appeared nearly six months after the murders, little more than an official notice that an estate sale of all items in a house listed at 1411 County Road. Everything in the house was to be liquidated in a sale the paper called "the final chapter in the Kellogg Murders," and which was to be conducted on behalf of Gloria Lynn Kellogg, "currently in residence at Daytonville."

Daytonville, I thought, the name like a bell ringing in my head, a little town in the far northeast corner of the state, known chiefly for the mental hospital that had long ago been established there, the name since then used like a threat by parents and teachers: *You better straighten up, boy, or they'll be sending you to Daytonville.*

"She must have had some kind of breakdown," I told my father when I got home later. "A pretty bad one if she had to be taken to Daytonville."

We were in the backyard, where I'd found him standing beside the sagging rusty fence that bordered it. He listened silently, taking long draws on his cigarette, peering at the tip as I went on, remaining silent even after I'd finished my account. For a time he stared at the copy of the notice I'd brought from the library, then he shook his head.

" 'On behalf,' " he said, quoting the paper. " 'The sale is to be conducted on behalf of Gloria Lynn Kellogg.' "

"Because she's in a mental hospital," I explained. "Because she had a breakdown of some sort."

My father thrust the notice back at me. "Unless it was just a way of getting control of things."

"What do you mean?"

"Porterfield," my father said. "He could have fixed it where he got control of things by putting Horace Kellogg's daughter in the

228

state asylum. He could have got control of things that way, everything that girl had."

This did not seem likely, and I said so. "Whatever Gloria had would have gone to her next of kin. But she'd have to be declared incompetent. That's a court matter. Out of Porterfield's control."

"Nothing was out of Porterfield's control," my father answered.

I saw another fiber grow in the tangled web my father had begun to weave.

"I remember that sale. They put everything out in the front yard. Had tags hanging off everything. Tables. Chairs. Lamps. A whole house full of furniture put out in the yard. And once they got everything sold, they had a big auction for the house."

"The Kellogg house was auctioned? When?"

" 'Bout two months after they sold everything that was in it," my father answered. He eyed me darkly. "Porterfield run the whole show that time. Set right up there with the auctioneer. I seen him settin' there when I drove by."

"What are you getting at, Dad?"

Rather than answering me directly, my father said, "They's something ain't right in all this, Roy. Something we ain't got to yet." He tossed the remainder of the cigarette across the fence, then drew another one from his pocket. "It's like a joke somebody's telling, only it ain't a joke, just works like one. You can't git none of it unless you git it all."

Another thought circled like a buzzard in his mind.

"Could be Porterfield had it all figured out even before them murders, Roy. What he'd do if something happened to Horace and his wife. How he could git his hands on what was theirs." He lit the cigarette and waved out the match. "He was always figuring like that. How to git his hands on other people's things. That's the way Porterfield is. Always plottin' things out. Settin' out there in that big yard of his. In that chair he's got. Year after year. Cold, hot. It don't never matter to him. He's always settin' there in the yard, figuring something out. Seen him many a time when I'd pass by."

"Why would you be passing by Wallace Porterfield's house?"

"On the way somewhere," he answered with a shrug.

"Wallace Porterfield's house isn't on the way to anything, Dad. It's at the end of a long road."

"When I went ridin' around, I'd pass by it sometimes." He smiled cunningly. "Bet Porterfield already had it figured out what he'd do if something happened to Horace Kellogg. Probably said, 'If he ever gets killed someway, this here is how I can get all he's got for my own-self.' "

"I don't think that's likely, Dad."

His eyes shot over to me almost angrily, as if I'd suddenly proven myself disloyal. "What's likely for a normal feller ain't got nothing to do with Wallace Porterfield."

His reaction was so fierce, I immediately retreated into a less aggressive form of reasoning. "Well, if Porterfield can plot things that far ahead, then he also has plenty of time to figure out how to cover his tracks."

"A man can't never cover everything though. They's always somebody looking. When your mama first got pregnant, seemed like the whole world got pregnant at the same time."

I stared at him blankly.

"They wasn't no more women pregnant than they'd ever been around here, but it seemed like it," he went on. "It's just that I hadn't noticed none of them before."

"Where are you going with this, Dad?"

"It's just one of them 'observations' you're always talking about, Roy. When something's on your mind, you notice things. Like pregnant women when your wife is pregnant. If something's gnawing at you, you notice everything that reminds you of it. Even over twenty years, it keeps gnawing. And so you keep noticing things. Little things or big things. It don't matter. Something about it don't let you rest."

His eyes narrowed and I saw that he was

coming to his point.

"Doc Poole," he said. "If they was something off about all this business with Gloria, he'd have noticed it. It would have kept on gnawing at him." He tapped the side of his emaciated skull. "Up here."

"I don't know, Dad, Doc Poole might —"

"What Porterfield said struck in Poole's craw. I bet other things stuck in it too. Things about Gloria, maybe."

"Yes, but . . ."

"You check with Poole, Roy," my father said in a tone that made it clear he would brook no argument.

I started to protest, but my father turned abruptly, like a general from a subordinate, the order given and thus beyond both refusal and appeal.

CHAPTER TWENTY-ONE

I didn't find Doc Poole at his office when I went there early the next morning.

A fat woman in a white uniform told me that he'd gone up to Waylord School, to a summer session where kids who'd been held back the year before could try again at the subjects they'd failed in hope of passing a test at the end of the summer and returning to school with their own class in the fall. It was something new, the nurse told me, started by Doc Poole and more or less subsidized by him.

"Doc's an old bachelor, you know," the woman said with a wry wink, "so he's got nothing better to spend his money on."

He was standing beneath the largely inadequate shade of a tall pine, when I reached the school an hour later. A group of children were playing in a dusty field not far away, dressed in the hand-me-down clothes of Waylord.

"Morning, Doc," I said as I came up beside him.

"Hey there, Roy." He was clearly surprised to see me, but there was also faint alarm in his expression. "Is it Jesse? You need me to —"

"No, no," I said hastily. "He's the same."

I glanced out over the field to where the children rushed about in the sweltering heat, boys in torn trousers, girls in faded shorts. It took only a slight turn of mind for me to imagine my father among them, dashing across the field to catch a tattered softball, a Waylord boy, with Waylord grit, determined to fight bare-knuckled to the end.

"They play hard, Waylord kids," I said.

"Yes, they do." Doc Poole kept his eyes on the field. "You never cared for sports, did you, Roy?"

"No, I tended to hole up in the library. It was my little fortress, I guess."

Doc Poole looked at me quizzically. "Against what?"

The answer occurred to me so swiftly, I must have known it all my life. "Against my father," I answered. "The library was the one place I knew he would never come to get me."

"Why not?"

"Because it intimidated him," I answered, surprised at how wily I'd been as a boy, how clever in the way I'd sought to best my father, to make him feel crude and inadequate. "I used to take books home just so he'd see them in my room. I used books like weapons. Threw them at him, like rocks."

Doc Poole watched me, a country doctor's long experience hovering in his wrinkled face.

"Coming home's not easy, is it, Roy?" he asked softly.

"You learn things, that's for sure."

He patted the empty metal chair beside him. "Take a load off. Watch the game awhile."

I looked out toward the field. "It hasn't changed much," I said, "the way things are up here."

"No, not much," Doc Poole agreed. "It was hard enough when the mine was going. When it closed, it just got worse."

"How'd you happen to settle here? In Kingdom County, I mean."

"I was born in Kingdom County," Doc Poole answered. "Came right back after medical school."

"You never thought of going anywhere else?"

"No," Doc Poole answered.

"It's all I thought about. Getting away. Living anyplace but here." I glanced to where a blackboard had been nailed to a tree, the parts of speech written out in yellow chalk. "Where's the teacher?"

"She left last week. Got a better offer in Welch. I'm looking for someone to take over next fall." He smiled. "Job's open if you want it."

I shook my head. "I've made my escape, Doc."

Doc Poole's eyes drifted back to me.

"What's on your mind, Roy? Why'd you drive all the way up here?"

"I mentioned what Porterfield said to you about the murders to my father and it got him thinking about things. He's pretty fired up. Wants to know all he can. The fact is, I don't really expect to find anything new. But I'm going through the motions. I went over the file on the case. I even talked to Porterfield himself, but I didn't get anything out of that." I offered a cold laugh. "Except that he believes my father came with Archie that night."

Doc Poole looked at me, astonished. "What?"

I waved my hand dismissively. "Anyway, my father wanted me to talk to you. He seems to think you may be able to help clear up a few things. About Gloria, in particular."

"Gloria?"

"Well, you were with her that morning, right?"

"Yes, I told her that her parents were both dead. That Archie had confessed to it all. She didn't say much of anything, as I recall." Doc Poole seemed to return to that distant morning, see again the small sunny room where he'd found Gloria hysterical in her bed. "I remember that she had her coat on. Even though she was under the covers. And little red rubber boots. Made me think if she'd just made it down the stairs and out

236

the door before Archie got inside, that, well, we wouldn't be sitting here right now talking about that night." He thought a moment, then added, "And she had a little gold locket in her hand. Wouldn't let go of it. Wallace finally pried it out of her fingers and dropped it in his pocket." He seemed to see the locket disappear into Porterfield's pocket. "Then he took Gloria over to his place. That's where she stayed after that. I offered to take her home, let her stay with me, but Wallace said it was up to him to see after her. He said he was her legal guardian."

"Porterfield took Gloria to his own house? Why?"

"Because he was her legal guardian."

"Porterfield was Gloria's legal guardian?"

Doc Poole smiled. "I was surprised by that myself. Wondered over it so much, I finally went down to the courthouse and looked it up. Turns out it was true. He'd been named Gloria's legal guardian just a few days after she was born. He was the executor of the estate too, so with Horace and his wife both dead, Wallace had to see after everything. Not only Gloria but . . ."

"Everything she owned," I said, repeating my father's words. "Why would Porterfield have been the executor of Horace Kellogg's estate?"

Doc Poole shrugged.

"Were he and Horace Kellogg close friends?"

"They may have been, but I didn't see them together all that often. I saw Wallace with Lavenia from time to time, but not much with Horace."

"With Lavenia?"

"That's right. She'd drop by the sheriff's office from time to time."

"Alone?"

"Sometimes with Gloria, but usually alone. When Gloria was a little girl, Lavenia sometimes left her there. In the office there with Wallace, I mean. She seemed to trust him."

"I didn't think anyone trusted Wallace Porterfield."

Doc Poole chuckled. "Everybody trusts someone, Roy. And I guess Lavenia, for whatever reason, felt that Wallace would take care of Gloria. Which he did, I guess. When she was a child, and later too, after the murders."

"Until he took her to Daytonville," I pointed out. "Why did he take her there?"

"Because she was in such bad shape. He couldn't take care of her anymore."

"What do you mean, 'bad shape'?"

"She kept trying to kill herself. After Archie, I mean. That's why Porterfield took her to Daytonville. So she could be looked after full-time."

"He had her committed?"

"Yes, he did," Doc Poole replied. "Gloria was sixteen, Roy. A minor. Wallace was her legal guardian."

"So he could just take her to the state asylum and leave her there?"

"Well, no, not exactly. It had to be certified. Gloria's condition. That she was a danger to herself. State law says a doctor has to do that. But once I signed the paper, Wallace could commit her."

"You certified Gloria?"

Doc Poole was silent a moment. Then, softly, he said, "Yes."

"Just on Porterfield's recommendation?"

"Not on that alone, no. But I had very much in mind the fact that Archie had killed himself not long before. Another young person dead, I didn't want that. There were already too many people dead in this thing. I sure didn't want Gloria added to the list."

"So she was definitely suicidal?"

"Wallace said she was," Doc Poole answered. "He keeps a gun cabinet in his living room. Full of pistols, rifles. Must have been twenty or thirty guns. He showed me where Gloria had tried to break into the cabinet. Desperate to get her hands on a gun. To use on herself, that's what Wallace said. She wanted to 'be with that boy,' as he put it."

"Did you examine Gloria?"

"Of course I did," Doc Poole answered. "But to tell you the truth, there wasn't much

239

to see when it came to Gloria. The whole time I tried to talk to her, she just sat at the dining room table there in Wallace's house. Head down. Hands in her lap. Pretty much out of it, as far as I could determine."

"Did she say anything?"

"I asked her a few questions. I'd never been asked to certify anybody before, and I figured that once she was in Daytonville, the people there would take a closer look at her. Professional people." He looked at me pointedly, so that I knew he was now coming to the real reason he'd acted so quickly in regard to Gloria's commitment. "The fact is, Gloria didn't need to be living in that house with Wallace Porterfield."

"Why?"

He seemed reluctant to answer, but after a moment his hesitancy was overcome, it seemed to me, by the demands of a larger truth. "Porterfield had a reputation, Roy. For liking . . . young girls. Teenage girls." He seemed vaguely embarrassed by the details. "He'd gotten a few in the family way. Usually poor girls, or girls who didn't have daddies or grown-up brothers to protect them. That's the type Wallace went after. Girls with relatives or boyfriends in trouble with the law. I never got the idea that he . . . did anything to Gloria, but I figured it was better to get her away from him. I mean, with his wife dead and Lonnie in the army, it was just the two of them in that house."

"So you signed the commitment papers."

"Yes," Doc Poole answered. "And Wallace took her right then." The old doctor appeared to see again what he'd seen that day, Porterfield slowly leading Gloria Kellogg to his car, placing her inside it, driving away. "Just put her in his patrol car and drove her to Daytonville."

"Did you ever see Gloria again?"

"One time," Doc Poole answered. "I drove up to Daytonville about two weeks later. She was in a bare room. Just a bed. Dressed in a hospital gown. She was pretty out of it. Drugged up, I think."

"How long did she stay there?"

"Maybe a month or so. I got a letter from Daytonville. It said that she'd been released."

"Released? To whom?"

"A woman. I don't remember her name, but they'd know who she was, the people over in Daytonville. You could go over and ask them about it."

"But would they be willing to tell me who she was?"

"Normally, no. But we'll work around that."

"How?"

Doc Poole smiled the smile of one who'd spent his life skirting bureaucratic hurdles. "I could tell them that you're working for me, the county coroner. That you're checking into something."

I looked at him doubtfully. "Into what?"

"Into what you really are looking into, Roy," Doc Poole replied. "An old murder case."

"Just got shed of her," my father said later that evening as we sat together at the supper table. The food on his plate was untouched. "Probably wasn't nothing wrong with Gloria 'cept Porterfield needed to get rid of her. So he brung her over to Daytonville and just left her to rot."

"But she really may have needed professional help, Dad," I countered. "It was Doc Poole who signed the papers, remember?"

This made no chink in the armor of my father's certainty.

"Just shipped her off when he was done with her," he insisted. "Shipped her off and kept it a secret. Locked her up so nobody would know where she was."

"People knew where Gloria was. It was in the paper, Dad. That she was in Daytonville."

"Didn't want nobody to know what he'd done," my father said as if he hadn't heard me, though I knew he had. "Must of had people down there working for him."

"Down where?"

"In the nuthouse," my father answered.

"Must have had somebody down there helping him out." He raised an empty fork, then lowered it. His eyes cut over to me. "Porterfield never did nothing without he thought it through first. So they had to be somebody in on it down there."

"In on what?"

"Whatever he was fixing to do," my father exclaimed. He appeared irritated with my denseness, the fact that the conspiracy was not as clear to me as it was to him. "Whatever he had to do to keep it all for hisself, Roy. Everything that would have gone to Horace Kellogg's daughter."

I smiled, but only as a way of covering the alarm I felt. "I think you're getting a little ahead of yourself, Dad," I said cautiously. "You don't have any real evidence that Wallace Porterfield was trying to get control of Gloria's inheritance."

My father ignited. "Well, he sold off the house, didn't he? That big old house and everything in it?" He gave a bitter snort. "Everybody figured he was doing it for Gloria. Selling it all, giving her the money. But he was doing it for hisself. And with Gloria locked up at Daytonville, he had a free hand. Wasn't nobody to stop him after that. Not once Gloria was out of the way."

"But she wasn't out of the way," I countered. "She was in Daytonville. But even then, she wasn't there for long. If Porterfield had really wanted Gloria out of the way, wouldn't he have kept her in Daytonville instead of allowing her to be released?"

"Released to some woman," my father said, repeating what I'd told him a few minutes before.

"That's right."

"Then that there woman must have been the one that was in on what Porterfield was up to," my father said triumphantly.

"There's no evidence Porterfield was up to anything, Dad." I sat back, stared at him, at the ire flashing in his eyes. "You hate Wallace Porterfield more than you ever hated anybody, don't you?"

He pushed his plate away, plucked a cigarette from the pack in his pocket. "He ain't fit to live, you ask me." He lit the cigarette and took a long draw, his gaunt face ringed in wisps of feathery smoke. "We got to find out what Porterfield done to Horace Kellogg's daughter. We got to go over to Daytonville and find out." He crushed the cigarette into the mound of mashed potatoes that rested, uneaten, on his plate. "I got at least that much left in me. The strength for one last trip."

I might have argued that he didn't, that the yellow had deepened in his eyes, that he no longer ate enough to sustain himself, that he was now in the last stage of his disease. I might have encouraged him to withdraw from this futile battle, seek, in the final days of his life, whatever serenity might be possible. But watching him at that moment, the way his eyes darted about, the twitching in his hands, I realized that it was not serenity my father longed for. It was the fire and sword of battle, the high hope of facing Wallace Porterfield as he had so many years before, repeating the words he'd blurted out then, *You're a liar. And a thief.*

CHAPTER TWENTY-TWO

And so, as we set out for Daytonville, I knew that this final trip was in some sense metaphorical, a last voyage taken with my father across the charred landscape of his youth. I looked at his crooked hands, smelled the odor of cigarettes in his skin and hair, and sensed the brutal, smoldering core of him, the wrong he'd suffered, distant and unrightable, but which he now sought beyond all reason to avenge. To get Wallace Porterfield was his only goal, the one blaze that still burned in him, and for which he seemed perfectly willing to devote whatever energy was left in him, the flame of retribution so greedy and voracious, so much the firestorm that propelled him, that I took it for the only one.

"I been thinking about something you told me," he said as we turned onto Route 6, the road that would finally wind its way through the mountains, then across a narrow valley, and terminate in Daytonville.

"What's that?"

"Porterfield that night," my father answered. "In Horace Kellogg's house. Was he in there a long time? By hisself, I mean. Before Doc Poole come by?"

"About thirty minutes, I guess," I said, trying to recall what Porterfield had written in his report.

"Thirty minutes," my father mused. "Wonder what he was doing all that time."

"It could have been anything, Dad. He went through the whole house, I imagine. And Gloria was in a terrible state. He probably spent a little time trying to calm her down before he called Doc Poole."

"Left Archie settin' outside in his car all that time. Handcuffed and just settin' there." He looked at me. "Never even called for Charlie Groom. That deputy he had back then. Don't that seem peculiar? Here he is, Sheriff Wallace Porterfield with two dead bodies, a girl clear out of her mind, and the guy that did the killing settin' in a car, and he don't call for no help. Don't call nobody for thirty minutes. Why not, Roy?" Before I could answer, he added, "Because he didn't want nobody in that house with him, that's why. Because he was up to something."

"Up to what?"

My father seemed annoyed by the question. "All I know is, Porterfield didn't call his deputy, and that seems mighty peculiar to me."

"Maybe his deputy was sick," I offered. "Or maybe he was out of town. You'd have to ask this Charlie Groom if you —"

"Charlie Groom's been dead ten years," he said.

"Were there any other deputies?"

"Not steady ones. If Porterfield needed help, he'd just call a guy in and deputize him. Like Lonnie done you, sending you after Lila. Getting you to help him find dirt on her."

"What makes you think he was trying to find dirt on Lila?"

"Maybe 'cause he wanted her for hisself," my father answered with a terrible certainty that he was right, that the Porterfields of Kingdom County sat on the satanic throne, pouring ruin into the cup from which all others drank. "Lila wouldn't pay Lonnie no mind. Went with you instead. So Lonnie wanted to get even with her. That's why he said that to her on the road. 'Cause he wanted to hurt her and make you look small."

And he had done that, I thought with a terrible sense that I'd fallen into the trap Lonnie Porterfield had set for me. Suddenly I found myself imagining life in the same way as my father imagined it, an evil agency sleepless at its core, forever plotting schemes of dark entrapment. It was not a vision of things I wanted to accept.

"I don't think Lonnie was ever interested in Lila," I said.

" 'Course he was," my father countered. "Lonnie knew you was aiming to marry Lila and he was jealous of that. That's why he yelled at her that night with you right beside her. So she'd have second thoughts."

There was no point in arguing the matter, so I said, "Well, one thing's for sure. I never had any second thoughts. Not about Lila. I just wanted to marry her and raise a family. That's all I wanted."

"I didn't know that, Roy," my father said. "That you wanted that more than anything."

"What did you think I wanted?"

"To get away," he answered. "Seemed like that was always on your mind. Getting away from . . . me."

I understood then how personally my father had taken my determination to leave Kingdom County, and thus how during all the time he'd watched me plot the route, he must have thought of it as a flight from himself.

"It wasn't anything against you," I said. "My needing to leave here."

My father nodded. "Didn't know that," was all he said.

We arrived at Daytonville State Asylum at just after one in the afternoon. By then my father looked considerably more weary than he had at the beginning of the trip. The long flight of stairs that led from the street to the building's high wooden entrance seemed beyond his power.

"I'd better just sit here in the shade," he said after I'd brought the car to a halt beneath a large oak. "You go on in."

Doc Poole had called ahead, and so I was quickly ushered into the office of Dr. William Spencer, who served, according to the sign posted on the door, as the asylum's administrative director.

Spencer was a short, middle-aged man with a rounded belly that spilled over the front of his trousers. He wore a light serge suit with the jacket unbuttoned, his pants held up by wide black suspenders. The degrees that hung from the wall behind his desk made it clear that he'd had a formidable education, medical school at Tulane, special training in psychiatry at Vanderbilt, and more postgraduate work at Emory in Atlanta. His tone was predictably professional and matter-of-fact.

"Dr. Poole says you work for the Coroner's Office," he said, offering his hand. "An investigator."

I nodded.

"And that you're looking into a murder case," Spencer went on. "The Kellogg murders." He waited for me to give a reason for this interest. When I didn't, he said, "Well, have a seat, Mr. Slater. I'll help you all I can." He picked up a folder that rested on the desk in front of him and handed it to me. "This is all the information I have on Gloria Kellogg. As you can see, it's pretty slim. Miss Kellogg was only here for a month or so. Not much time to get to know her. Psychologically speaking, I mean."

There'd been only one formal report, I noticed as I flipped through the pages of the file.

"L. P. Mitchell," I said, glancing at the name signed at the bottom of it.

"Dr. Mitchell, yes," Spencer said. "He was in charge of the hospital in those days."

"Where is he now?"

"Dr. Mitchell retired not long after Miss Kellogg was released," Spencer answered. "He lived to quite a ripe old age, but unfortunately he died two years ago."

"Did you ever talk to Gloria Kellogg?" I asked.

"As a matter of fact, I did. I was right out of college. Dr. Mitchell was my boss at the time. He sent me in to see Miss Kellogg. Pretty much a test, as he told me. Of my powers of observation."

"What did you observe?"

"Extreme withdrawal," Spencer replied. "She was correctly oriented, as we say, to time and place. She wasn't hallucinating. But beyond that, if you don't mind a vulgar phrase, there was nobody home." He shrugged. "Of course, I saw her for only a few minutes on the day she was admitted.

Dr. Mitchell spent more time with her after that, but it was not a case I recall ever discussing with him." He glanced at his watch. "I'm sorry to rush, but I have to see a patient in another wing." He rose. "Take as long as you like to look over the file. If you need to talk to me again, let me know, but to tell you the truth, Mr. Slater, I really don't have any more information on this matter." He shook my hand again, walked to the door, then turned. "By the way, wasn't the boyfriend executed?"

I saw my brother as Wallace Porterfield must have seen him the morning he came back down the corridor to Archie's cell, a body dangling from the bars, head down, face blackened.

"No," I said. "The boyfriend hung himself."

Something rose in Spencer's mind. "Had that already happened when Gloria came here?"

"Yes, it had."

He considered this for a moment, then said, "I suppose that's why she was kept on suicide watch, then. Not only what she'd been through, but the fear that she might have entered into some kind of death pact with her boyfriend. Teenagers do that sort of thing, you know." He shrugged. "Well, like I said, take as long as you want with the file."

With that, he stepped from the room and

closed the door, leaving me alone.

The admission form of Daytonville State Asylum was the first paper in the file.

According to its record, Wallace Porterfield had arrived with Gloria at ten o'clock on the morning of February 15, 1964. At that time Gloria's possessions had been carefully inventoried. They'd consisted of a small suitcase, two nightdresses, a bag of toiletries complete with soap, toothbrush, toothpaste, and shampoo. Gloria had also packed several blouses, a wool sweater, and two pairs of denim jeans. She'd worn a watch, which was taken from her, presumably because its metal band was considered dangerous. She'd also brought along the gold locket Doc Poole had mentioned to me and which upon admission was also taken from her.

By ten-thirty, according to the admission form, Gloria had changed into the pale blue dress mandated by the asylum, and had been taken to Room 316 in an upstairs ward designated as "Secure."

Briefly, I tried to imagine the girl I'd known, Archie's girl, sitting alone on a stripped mattress, facing the bare plaster walls of the Daytonville State Asylum. I saw her thin body draped in the blue institutional dress, her hair falling uncombed to her shoulders, her eyes locked in the terrible inwardness she'd fallen into since that snowy night when she'd waited for my brother to come for her, claim her, sweep her away to distant Nashville. Never had she seemed more lost to me, more frail, more completely and eternally destroyed.

And yet there was far worse in store for Gloria, a fate duly recorded in her file, and which I asked Spencer about when he returned to the room an hour later.

"They gave her Haldol," I said. "That's a pretty powerful drug." I glanced at the file. "It probably made her condition much worse."

Spencer returned to the chair behind his desk. "No one knew that at the time, of course. I'm sure Dr. Mitchell believed that it was in Gloria's best interest, given her condition."

"How would you describe her condition?"

"Stricken," Spencer answered. "I believe that's the word I used in my note to Dr. Mitchell. You no doubt read it in the file there."

"Stricken by guilt. That's what you wrote."

"The guilt she felt for what happened. The murders. Particularly her father."

"Why her father?"

"Because he suffered so much. Evidently he was shot quite a few times. Of course, it was Gloria's boyfriend who'd actually murdered her father, but she blamed herself anyway."

"Did she say anything else about the murders?"

"No."

"How about the boyfriend?"

He shook his head. "We never got around to talking about him."

"Why not?"

"Well, for one thing, her guardian came into the room and she got very quiet after that."

"Her guardian. Wallace Porterfield."

"Yes," Spencer said. "He sat down on the bed beside her, and the two of them just sat there until I left the room. I don't believe I ever spoke to her again."

"Why not?"

"Because she was Dr. Mitchell's patient," Spencer replied. "I'd see her in the dayroom from time to time, of course, but I never talked to her again."

"Did Porterfield ever show up again?"

"Not that I know of. At least, not until that last day. The day Miss Kellogg left."

I glanced down at the file. "Gloria was released to a woman named Mavis Wilde. Do you know who she is?"

"No, I don't," Spencer answered. "But I know she came with Sheriff Porterfield that morning. When Gloria was taken out of the hospital."

I flipped through the file until I came to the release form. "In the place marked 'Relationship,' somebody wrote 'Friend.'"

"Then presumably Miss Wilde was a friend of Gloria's."

"The file also says that she took Gloria to her own home," I added. "In Pittsville. Was she young? Old?"

"Young," Spencer answered immediately. "In her twenties, I'd say. Something like that. She was certainly a good deal younger than Sheriff Porterfield."

"Do you remember anything else about her?"

"No. It was Porterfield who left a vivid impression. Partly his size, I suppose, but his authority too. He seemed in charge of everything. The woman was merely someone who worked for him. Or at least, that was the impression I got. That she worked for him. Not professionally. Not in the sheriff's department. But privately. In some low capacity."

"Low capacity?"

"Well, she wasn't dressed like a professional person. Rather gaudy, as I recall. Big plastic earrings. That sort of thing." Spencer laughed. "Of course, she may not have been wearing plastic earrings at all, but she gave off that sort of impression. So this morning, when I read in Gloria's file that the woman was from Pittsville, it didn't surprise me."

"What do you mean?"

"They have a women's prison there," Spencer said. "Mavis Wilde struck me as the sort of person who could easily have been familiar with the 'inner workings' of a place like Pittsville."

★ ★ ★

"She was in on it, that woman," my father snarled when I described the same scene to him a few minutes later. "Porterfield probably give her part of what he stole from Gloria." His eyes flared with contempt. "Bought and sold, that woman. Bought and sold by Porterfield."

The rabid nature of his response — his certainty that Mavis Wilde could be nothing more than one of Wallace Porterfield's evil minions — gave no room for argument, so I offered none, but waited, certain that if I kept quiet, he would go on to another issue.

"It's the Haldol that's the point, if you ask me," he blurted out after a moment. "That's the reason Porterfield brought that girl all the way over here. To get her out of the way. Drug her up. So he could get his hands on everything she had and people wouldn't know what he was up to."

He was now more convinced than ever that Wallace Porterfield had somehow profited from the murders of Horace and Lavenia Kellogg, reaped advantage from the very act that had destroyed his son, the fire burning so hot in him, he seemed almost entirely consumed by it.

"Porterfield was always grabbing for things," he added. "Back in Waylord, he'd have some old shack condemned, drive the people out of it, then buy it hisself." His face

257

jerked into a scowl. "It's in Porterfield's blood to grab things. But this time it wasn't just some old shack in the hills. It was a big, fine house. Must have set Porterfield's mouth to watering."

"The trouble is," I reminded him gently, "everything Horace Kellogg had went to Gloria."

"So he had that doctor drug her up," my father said. "Had him fix it so Gloria couldn't never think for herself. That way he could grab everything. Do it all legal too. Just say he had to take over 'cause Gloria didn't have no sense."

In his rage, my father seemed half mad now, half insane with his need to exact revenge on Wallace Porterfield. And yet, as I had to admit, there was reason in what he said, and logic too, a fearsome plausibility at every stage of the argument, so that in the slanted light I could see it all as my father saw it, Porterfield's evil purpose carefully calculated and coldly carried out. All I had to do was imagine Porterfield as my father did, a man beyond human dimension, an evildoer of gargantuan appetite, with his pistol and his badge fully arrayed in diabolical majesty, a conscienceless destroyer of the poor, the weak, all the malignancy of man festering in his vile heart.

Then, as if to stretch Porterfield's imperial malice to the breaking point, my father said,

"You know, it could be Archie never left his car, Roy."

I stared at him, stunned.

"Maybe it was Porterfield in that house. Doing it all hisself. The murders. Ain't nothing Porterfield wouldn't do if they was something he wanted."

"But what about the gun?" I reminded him, for the first time actually unnerved by my father's extremity, the perilous swamp of fantasy into which he had now sunk. "Archie brought that gun, and it was the murder weapon."

"How do you know for sure it was really that gun that done it?"

To my surprise, I had to admit that I didn't know for sure that my father's gun had been the weapon used that night.

My father pounced. "See what I mean?" he demanded. "We just took it for the truth. Everything Porterfield said."

"But Archie said some things too, Dad. He confessed, remember? And not just to Porterfield. To me."

"Could have been Archie got scared and just up and said them things," he said. "Maybe he would have took it back. Maybe that's why . . ." His eyes widened. "Maybe that's why he's dead, Roy, 'cause he was about to take it all back."

The mad flame leapt again, hot and wild. "You got to find Gloria, Roy," he declared with the insane certainty of one who could no longer entertain a separate reality, nor give the slightest credence to a world other than the one smoldering in his mind. "She's the only living witness. You got to find her and make her tell the truth."

CHAPTER TWENTY-THREE

I waited until I'd heard the last of his movements behind the door, the final agitated twist and turn of his body in the tangled sheets, then the long, heavy exhalation of breath that signaled that he'd passed into unconsciousness at last. Then I crept to where the telephone rested on a small wooden table in the living room and called Doc Poole.

"Something wrong, Roy? You sound —"

"It's my father, he's —"

"I'll be right over."

"No, wait," I said hastily. "It's not physical exactly. Well, maybe it is, I don't know. That's why I'm calling, I guess."

"What is it, Roy? What's the matter with Jesse?"

"He seems . . . crazy."

From the sound of his voice, and the steady nature of his response, this did not appear to surprise Doc Poole in the least.

"What's he doing? Tell me exactly."

"He's got this idea in his head. Lots of ideas, really, but they're all connected to one thing. He's absolutely certain that Porterfield is behind everything. The Kellogg murders. Archie's suicide. Gloria's institutionalization."

I waited for a response, then added, "It's my fault. I should never have started looking into it."

"It's nobody's fault," Doc Poole assured me. "It's dementia. He could have had a little stroke."

"What can I do?" I asked, and heard the helplessness in my voice.

"Not much, unless you want to . . . calm him down."

"I don't want to drug him, Doc. These are the last days of his life. I want him to live them . . . aware."

"Then you'll just have to play along with him, Roy," Doc Poole said. "You could argue with him, but it wouldn't do any good. He'd fight you tooth and nail, and after a while you two probably wouldn't even be speaking to each other again. So you just have to climb into his mind. Play along with whatever crazy stuff he comes up with."

I tried to do exactly that as I lay sleepless in bed a few hours later. I tried to climb into my father's mind, search through it as if it were the charred ruin of a devastated house. I went over all his theories about what Wallace Porterfield had done, judged each as utterly unproved, even beyond proof. And the more I weighed the facts, the more obvious it became that the facts themselves did not matter to my father. But this truth only led to a final question: How would I be measured as a son if I didn't join my father in this doomed quest to bring Wallace Porterfield to his knees?

I knocked softly at his door, carried the breakfast I'd prepared into him, nothing more than a single hard-boiled egg and black coffee, all he could get down.

"I've decided to do it," I told him as I set the tray on his lap.

He stared listlessly at the egg and coffee. His hand moved toward neither one.

"I'm going to look for Gloria."

He nodded wearily, the exertions of the day before now taking a terrible toll upon whatever reserves of strength he still possessed. "You got to find her, Roy," he said, his voice barely above a whisper. "She knows what Porterfield done."

"If he did anything," I cautioned in a final hesitation before I took the plunge.

The old eyes leapt toward me. "Oh, he done something, all right. And he has to pay for what he done." His half-curled fingers shook in the boiling air between us. "Otherwise . . . otherwise there ain't . . ." He stared at me pleadingly. "Otherwise, they ain't no use, Roy." His head sank. His voice lowered. "No use to nothing on this earth."

That was when I saw it plainly, the true quest of my father. I had been wrong. It wasn't revenge he sought. It was *meaning*. Wallace Porterfield had to be guilty of something, and he had to be punished for it, not because my father wanted to avenge himself, but because he needed, powerfully and achingly, for the world to make sense.

And so I said, "I have a plan."

My father lifted his head slowly.

"For finding Gloria. I got it from some detective novel I read years ago. I'm not sure it'll work in real life, but there's no harm in trying it."

I waited for a response, but none came. Instead, my father drew in a long, heavy breath.

"I'm going to call Wallace Porterfield, and when he answers, I'm going to whisper a name. Mavis Wilde. Then I'm going to drive to Porterfield's house and see if he gets in that big Lincoln of his."

"Follow him if he does?" my father asked.

I nodded. "In the hope that he'll lead me right to Mavis Wilde. From her, maybe I can get to Horace Kellogg's daughter."

My father nodded approvingly, though I'm sure he could see the same gigantic holes in the plan that were completely apparent to me. Porterfield could do nothing. Or he could simply call Mavis Wilde on the telephone. After so many years he might not even recognize her name.

"It may not work, of course," I admitted as I rose and headed for the phone.

But, to my astonishment, it did.

The drive was almost seventy miles, and Porterfield drove it slowly through the rain, with an old man's caution. From time to time he would nod to an approaching car, or wave to someone he recognized in one of the stunted towns through which we passed. But he never stopped, never veered, and in that steady, determined movement, I sensed an equally steady and determined purpose, so that I grew increasingly confident that the old sheriff was in fact leading me to Mavis Wilde, and that in finding her I would discover not only Porterfield's crime, but something dark at the heart of my family's life, the wellspring of our undoing — my father's, Archie's, mine — a place whose existence was curiously mirrored by where Porterfield led me, deeper and deeper into the woods, almost, it seemed to me, into a forest primeval.

Another twenty minutes passed before Porterfield finally turned into a muddy driveway, then brought his car to a halt before a small wooden house, remote and desolate, so nearly engulfed by the surrounding woods it seemed itself a kind of weed.

I swept past the house, drove on a few hundred yards, then turned back and drew close enough to keep an eye on it through a gap in the trees.

The Lincoln rested like a gleaming stone in

front of the house. I could see Porterfield sitting behind the wheel, one hand in his lap, the other rising and falling rhythmically as he brought a cigarette to his mouth then drew it away again. I watched the gray smoke curl out of the open window, Porterfield nearly motionless, slouched in a heaviness that struck me as curiously melancholy, and which gave him the appearance of a man who in some deeply fundamental way was no friend to himself.

I don't know exactly how long I waited, watching trails of rain streak down the windshield, only that I had nearly come to the conclusion that Porterfield had driven to this remote place for no better reason than to sit inside his big black car, smoking silently, adrift in ancient fears, as I imagined, an old lawman doomed to remain on stakeout forever, and that none of it, not one inch of the long drive from Kingdom City, had had anything to do with my phone call or the name I'd pronounced with a sinister whisper in Porterfield's ear.

Then a muddy blue sedan suddenly appeared in the distance. It slowed as it neared the driveway, then made a wide turn. As it turned, I saw a woman behind the wheel, her face obscured by rain and fog. She drove up beside Porterfield and got out. I leaned forward, tried to determine if this could be the vulgar, dark-haired woman Dr. Spencer had glimpsed in the lobby at Daytonville, but her head was covered by a bloodred hat, her body by a yellow slicker. And so I could make out nothing about her except that she walked through the sheeting rain with a determined stride, giving no notice to the old white dog that suddenly pranced up beside her, then tagged behind for a few feet before drifting away again. Instead, she continued on until she reached the passenger door of Porterfield's car, opened it, and got inside.

I waited, able to see no more than faint smudges behind the Lincoln's foggy windows, the occasional curl of smoke that swept up from the driver's side when a window was cracked to let it out.

A few minutes later, the passenger door opened again. The woman emerged from the car, bent against the rain. She gave a quick nod, then slammed the door. Stepping back, she watched, her back to me, as Porterfield pulled away.

I waited until the Lincoln's red taillights had disappeared into the mist before I turned into the driveway. I heard my father's voice in my mind, *Oh he done something, all right,* and for the first time I believed him, believed that through the years Wallace Porterfield and Mavis Wilde had been partners in a criminal collusion, hiding Gloria Kellogg from the world, along with all she must have known about what really happened after my brother brought his battered old Ford to a halt behind the tall dark hedge.

I'd completely embraced the reality of their conspiracy by the time I reached the door of the cabin, accepted it fully, completely, and with the kind of certainty we can feel only when we have come to believe that we will indeed confront the secret scheme that steals our happiness away, make it deal a few last cards face up.

CHAPTER TWENTY-FOUR

The first card turned abruptly when the door opened to my knock, the face upon it hard and brittle, with matted, unwashed hair. I guessed her age at around fifty, though she might easily have been ten years older. And yet, I had no doubt I knew who now stood before me in the doorway. There were no plastic earrings, no cheap costume jewelry, but the essential nature of Spencer's description remained fully visible in the predatory gleam of her dark eyes. There was something low about her, and it struck me that this baseness was the soil from which she'd sprung and in which she was truly and eternally rooted. Time might remold the features of her face, pluck the plastic earrings from her ears, but she would remain forever what she had forever been: a wholly purchased soul.

"Mavis Wilde," I said then, when she remained silent. "My name's Roy Slater. I'm —"

"I know who you are," the woman said.

Her face was narrow, shrunken, so that she looked curiously mummified, eyes and mouth little more than holes cut clumsily out of a leather sack.

"Wallace said you might show up here.

Said you called his house this morning. Said my name and hung up."

"How'd he know it was me?"

She grinned mockingly. "There's ain't much Wallace don't know." The grin twisted from mockery to amusement. "He drove slow so you wouldn't lose him."

"Porterfield likes playing with people."

She eyed me silently, taking my measure, but without fear, so that I sensed that she'd faced down a lifetime of threatening men. "Wallace said you was all stirred up about them murders. The ones your brother done."

"I'm looking into it."

She stared at me as if she were trying to decide whether to hear me out or close the door in my face, able to do either with equal indifference.

"Well, you might as well come in, Roy Slater. It's been a long time since a man set foot in this old place."

I stepped into the house and peered about the room. The water-stained wallpaper had peeled away like a leper's skin and the scarred floor was scattered with old magazines, piles of yellowing newspaper.

"I ain't got around to pitching all this stuff out," Mavis said. "Tried to sell this place, but way out here in the boonies, ain't no buyers." She slumped down on a faded red sofa, then slung her legs up onto the pocked wooden table that stretched before it. "It ain't too smart, fooling with Wallace, you know. He don't like people poking into his private business."

"Was this place one of his 'private businesses'?"

She cackled loudly. "You might say we did some business. You ain't never been in a cathouse before, have you, Roy, honey?"

"No, I haven't."

She plucked a purse from the table, grabbed a pack of cigarettes from it. "Well, ain't that pitiful," she said, and cackled again. "This little place used to be full of boys. Mostly from the army base they used to have 'bout fifteen miles from here. Different bunch of boys every night. Come from everywhere, them boys. Every part of the country." She let her gaze drift about the room. "I had five, six girls working here." Her eyes settled upon me. "Don't look so surprised by my telling you all this. I ain't hiding nothing. I done my time for running this place, so I ain't got no reason to be afraid of you." She lit the cigarette. "Besides, I never seen nothing wrong in it. Hell, we had plenty of boys just like you come over here. Come all the way from Kingdom City. Looking for a little . . . experience." Her eyes narrowed into small reptilian slits. "But you didn't come all the way from Kingdom County to hear about my glory days, did you?"

"No."

"Come over here about them murders. That's what Wallace told me. That you got it in your head your brother didn't kill them people."

"That's right."

"Wallace said if you showed up, I ought to ask you a question." The grin returned, a mocking challenge. "Who done it? That's what Wallace told me to ask you. If your brother didn't do it, then who did? Wallace said to ask you that, see what you said."

"I don't have to jump through a hoop for Wallace Porterfield," I answered, an anger as fierce and terrible as my father's flashing through me. "He's not going to play with me anymore."

"He ain't playing with you." Mavis said it firmly. "At least, not much. If Wallace was really playing with you, honey, you'd know it."

"Well, he tried to make me believe that my father had something to do with the murders," I told her. "Two sets of footprints, he said. Coming from my brother's car. He said one of those sets belonged to my father."

"Maybe it did."

"No, it didn't."

Mavis peered at me for a moment, then said, "Well, don't none of it matter to me anyway." She leaned forward and crushed the cigarette into a dirty glass. "I don't know nothing about them murders. Happened all the way over in Kingdom County. Heard about 'em, but that's all." She sank back against the stained cushions, her eyes bright with malice. "Wallace said you'd be asking about Gloria. Said you wouldn't never heard of me if you hadn't been snooping around, asking questions about that girl. Well, go ahead. Whatever questions you got, ask them. Then get on back home 'cause I ain't got no more business with you."

"You came with Porterfield to Daytonville the day he picked up Gloria?"

"Sure did." She laughed cheerlessly. "But, hell, they ain't no mystery to that. Wallace needed help, that's all. In getting Gloria. So I come along with him."

"Why did he need your help?"

"To take care of her after he took her out of that nuthouse she was in. He needed somebody to look after her for a while."

"Why you?"

" 'Cause he trusted me. All those years he come over here. We had a little arrangement. While he was sheriff, I mean. All that time, I never told a soul."

"He was one of your . . . customers?"

"No, Wallace didn't never want no whore," Mavis said. "He always brought his own girl with him. He just needed a place to bring her, that's all. Out of Kingdom County, I mean. Private. Him being the law over there and all." She slung her arm over the back of the sofa and grinned. "You ever just needed a place, Roy?"

"Where did you take Gloria when you left Daytonville that day?"

Mavis dragged a skinny hand through the matted curls of her hair. "Brung her home with me. And seen after her real good too. In my own house. Not here. I got another place in Pittsville. That's where Gloria stayed. A nice place, where I could see after her proper, or make sure somebody kept an eye on her if I was gone. Girl couldn't do nothing for herself. I mean, she wasn't no cripple or nothing. She could walk around, talk to you. Stuff like that. Just didn't have no get-up-and-go. But she had to be watched. Wallace was real firm about that." Afraid she'd kill herself.

I heard my father's voice: *Probably wasn't nothing wrong with Gloria, 'cept Porterfield wanted to get rid of her.* "Are you sure of that?" I asked.

To my surprise, she seemed offended by my doubt. " 'Course I'm sure. Ain't no reason for Wallace to have told me nothing like that if he didn't believe it. That was why he took her to Daytonville in the first place. 'Cause he couldn't keep her from bumping herself off and run Kingdom County at the same time."

"Maybe he just wanted to get rid of her."

Mavis snorted. "Oh yeah? Well, let me tell

you something — if Wallace Porterfield wanted to get rid of that girl, he'd have got rid of her. They wouldn't be no driving her over to Daytonville. Talking to all them doctors. Or taking her out again and putting her with me. And I'll tell you something else while I'm at it: Long as I had charge of Gloria, she was well took care of."

"How long did you 'have charge' of her"?

"Couple months, that's all. Wallace paid me good for it too. But she was a whiny little thing. Money or not, I was glad to see her go."

"Go?" I asked, now aware that I might have to follow those lost steps too, but which I felt utterly resolved to do. Gloria had become to me some frail child out of a dark fairy tale, bewildered, wandering lost in the forest, dropping bread crumbs in a futile attempt to leave a trail.

"Yeah, Wallace sent her down south." Mavis struggled to her feet, walked to a small table, and retrieved a single white envelope. "Wallace brought me this letter when he come over this morning. He said to give it to you since you seemed so all fired up about knowing what happened to Gloria."

"He thinks of everything, doesn't he?" I asked stiffly.

"Yeah, he does." Mavis's voice was metallic. "Here. Read it. And then git gone. I ain't got no more time to fool with you."

The letter was from a place called Bryce

Treatment Center, located in Baton Rouge, Louisiana. It stated that on June 9, 1974, Gloria Lynn Kellogg, age 26, had died of a brain aneurism. As Miss Kellogg's "only living relative," Wallace Porterfield was assured that everything possible had been done for her, and was asked to make the necessary funeral arrangements.

"Why does this say that Porterfield is Gloria's only living relative?" I asked.

" 'Cause he was."

"I don't believe you," I said.

"I don't care whether you do or not," Mavis snapped. "But I know for a fact Wallace and Gloria's mother was cousins. That's why she come to Kingdom County in the first place, 'cause Wallace said he'd put her husband on as a deputy."

"Where was the rest of her family?"

"Wallace never said. Told me he was stuck with Gloria, 'cause her mother was his cousin. That nobody else would lift a finger for her, so it was up to him to see after her. Which he did."

I felt a small thread snap in the elaborate fabric of conspiracy my father had woven so persuasively.

"Fact is, Wallace done what he could for Gloria," Mavis said. "Spent a fortune on her. Keeping her in that hospital down south. Cost him a whole hell of a lot of money to do that."

"But it wasn't his money," I argued, determined to stitch the tapestry up again, make it tough and strong, able to bear the weight of my father's anguished need to bring logic to the universe. "Porterfield used Gloria's money to —"

"Gloria's money?" A laugh rattled from Mavis's twisted mouth. "Gloria didn't have no money."

"Of course she did," I said emphatically. "The money she inherited. From her father."

Mavis's laugh jangled again. "Gloria's daddy was a thief. Give hisself big loans from his own bank. It all had to be paid back. That damn girl didn't have a penny."

"But the house and everything in it," I persisted, conjuring up my father's description of the auction, people gathered in the wide front yard, bidding on furniture, dishes, finally the riches of the house itself, Porterfield in charge of it all, watching greedily as Gloria's patrimony was sliced into pieces and carted away.

"Wallace had to sell off everything," Mavis informed me. "They was big people had a stake in that bank. They had to be paid back or it would all have got out about Gloria's daddy. So Wallace paid them. Time it was over, there wasn't a penny left for nothing." She laughed. "Wallace used to say your brother done that no-account daddy of Gloria's a favor by shooting him. Said Horace

Kellogg would have ended up in the penitentiary pretty soon anyway. Said he got what he deserved when your brother killed him."

Which, as I realized, had finally brought me full circle, back to the reason I'd whispered Mavis's name in Porterfield's ear, back to that snowy night twenty years before, the wild shots that had rung out behind the ornate door of 1411 County Road.

"Did Gloria ever talk to you about the murders?" I asked.

"She had this old locket. Said her grandmother give it to her. It brought things back when she fiddled with it."

"Things?"

"Just got her to whining over it," Mavis answered. "Said she had to have the damn locket 'cause she was gonna hock it. When they got away, I mean. Her and that boyfriend of hers, your brother. Anyway, Gloria said he didn't have no money so she was gonna take that locket to wherever they went once they got away. That's all she ever said about them killings. Just how, come hell or high water, she had to have that damn locket, and she aimed to get it no matter what he said."

"What who said?"

"Her boyfriend, I guess," Mavis answered. "The one she was running off with. He didn't want her to get that locket, but Gloria said she had to have it, and she wasn't going to leave without it."

"But she *did* have it," I said, baffled. "She had it when Porterfield found her that night."

Mavis shrugged. "All I know is she had to have it. That's what Gloria told me. That she had to have that locket and she wasn't going to let him stop her. Said they fought about it 'cause he didn't want her to go get it."

Go get it. I felt something shift in my mind, saw Archie's car parked beside the hedge, two people in the front seat, arguing desperately. *I have to have it, Archie. No. I'm going back for it. Gloria, don't. I have to have it!* Then the door of my brother's old black Ford opened, Gloria racing out into the night, turning up the driveway, leaving the tracks in the snow that Wallace Porterfield had later seen.

"Did Gloria say what happened after she went back for the locket?" I asked.

"Just that she went to her room to get it, and she had it right in her hand when all hell broke loose downstairs. All this screaming, she said. Her mother screaming for her father, telling him that this boy had a gun."

I heard my brother's anguished apology, *I didn't mean for her to see it.*

Lavenia Kellogg, I thought, imagining Archie's panic as Horace Kellogg rushed toward him. *So fast.* Rushed into the room and saw the pistol, turned and ran toward where he hoped to find his own. *So fast.* A woman fleeing up the stairs. *So fast.* A man running down a corridor. *So fast.* And so no time to think, to argue, to explain, no time to do anything but reach for the pistol they'd already seen and with it stop the screaming and the panic, the chaos and the terror, the wild rush of time, because everything was happening . . . *so fast.*

"Oh, Archie," I whispered.

Mavis toyed absently with her hair. "Well, you got any more questions?"

"No," I answered. Now I knew, accepting the fact that Wallace Porterfield had had nothing whatsoever to do with my brother's death, nor the murders themselves, nor ever connived to gain advantage from either of them. He had "played" with me, the old devil in him bent on tormenting me, but he was innocent of the deaths that had wrecked my family's life.

"That's it, then?" Mavis asked.

The gavel fell. Case closed, I thought, on Wallace Porterfield.

"Yes," I said.

"Good," Mavis said. " 'Cause Wallace figured you was after him."

"I was," I admitted.

Mavis snorted. "I'm surprised ain't nobody ever come after him before you," she said, her voice filled with admiration for the aging sheriff, the evil he'd done yet always managed to escape. " 'Course, Wallace had a way of scaring people so they wouldn't tell." She laughed. "Especially them girls he brought here." She walked to a cabinet, drew out a bottle of whiskey, and poured herself a drink. "Brought in for questioning, he called it."

Doc Poole's voice sounded in my mind, *Betty said he took Lila in for questioning.*

"Did you ever see any of these girls?" I asked.

Mavis took a swig. "Seen 'em all."

"Did you ever see a girl with bright red hair?"

Mavis set down her glass. "Red hair?" She laughed again, but mirthlessly. "No, I didn't never see no girl with red hair." She glanced away, her eyes squeezing together slightly as if trying to bring that very girl into focus, the one she hadn't seen. "You better be on your way. I ain't got no more time for this."

"A girl with red hair," I repeated coldly. "Brought in for questioning."

Mavis walked to the sofa, snatched up the yellow slicker, and began to put it on. "I don't remember no girl with red hair. Come on now, I got to go."

My father's accusation leapt from my mouth. "You're a liar."

Mavis stepped to the door and opened it. "Get out of here now."

I didn't move. "Porterfield brought a girl

here. She had red hair. Her name was Lila Cutler."

Mavis watched me tensely, her body rigid, eyes defiant. "I ain't telling you nothing."

I felt something rise, fierce and newly born in me, my father's ancient rage. "What did he do to her?"

"He didn't do nothing," Mavis snarled. "Get out of here!"

I strode across the room, grabbed the door, slammed it, then grabbed Mavis Wilde by the throat and squeezed with a violence that seemed to build with each passing second.

Mavis's eyes bulged, her face fixed in animal terror. She was gasping for air, but I didn't care. "He said she wasn't worth the fight." She gasped. "Said she wasn't even *fresh*."

My fingers bit into her throat. "Tell it all."

"I thought he'd gone too far this time." Mavis's fingers clawed at my hand. "The way she fought him. I thought, 'He's gonna have to kill her 'cause that one ain't gonna take it. She's gonna tell for sure what he done to her.' But he started telling her how he had the goods on her boyfriend. He said, 'You keep your mouth shut about this if you want that boyfriend of yours to stay alive. 'Cause I can arrest him anytime I want to.' That's what Wallace told her. That she either keep her mouth shut or he'd make sure that boyfriend of hers paid for it good."

I released Mavis Wilde's throat and she sank to the floor, sucking in great gulps of air. "I guess she never said nothing about what he done," she gasped, " 'cause nobody never come over here looking to make Wallace pay."

Betty Cutler's condemnation cut through my mind, *You're not the man your daddy was.*

True enough, I thought. *Until now.*

CHAPTER TWENTY-FIVE

My father's eyes fluttered open as I slammed into his room. He saw the rage in my face, the steaming wave I rode.

"Roy? What happened?"

I jerked open the door of his closet. "Porterfield."

He stirred on the bed, kicking at the sheets. "What are you looking for?"

"This."

He stared at the rifle in alarm. "What's got into you?"

"Where are the shells?"

"Put that gun down."

He lifted himself to a sitting position, then drew his legs over the rumpled side of the bed.

"Put it down, Roy."

I jerked open the top drawer of his bureau, the place he'd always kept his bullets in the past, and there it lay, a box of shells nestled among his socks and underwear.

"Roy, stop it," my father said. "Gimme that gun."

I opened the breech and shoved a bullet into the cylinder. "Wallace Porterfield is going to pay."

I started for the door, but with an unexpected burst of energy, my father staggered forward and blocked my path. "Roy, give me that goddamn gun."

"Get out of my way, Dad."

For a moment, our eyes locked. Then my father stepped aside to let me pass.

I turned toward the door, heard my father rustle behind me, then a groan, like someone lifting a crushing weight, and after that, blackness.

I didn't know how much time had gone by before I saw light again. My eyes opened, then closed, then opened again, a space of murky shadows. Minutes passed, and the shadows fled, the room now illuminated by a blinding shaft of sunlight.

I lay facedown on the floor, and it took me some time to realize that I was still in my father's bedroom. Everything was silent, and in that silence I remembered the way I'd turned from my father, the sound of his groan, but it was only when I saw Archie's baseball bat on the bed that I realized what he'd used.

Woozily, I staggered to my feet and looked around for the rifle. It wasn't there. I stumbled out of the room, rubbing the knot at the back of my skull, and peered out the front window.

He was sitting silently on the old orange sofa behind me, the rifle in his lap.

"You all right?" he asked.

When I only glared at him, he said, "I had to stop you, Roy."

"You haven't stopped me," I said, the rage building again, fired by a terrible image of Lila on her back, Porterfield's massive bulk rising and falling above. "I'm going to make him pay, Dad."

I strode across the room and yanked the rifle from his hand.

"Roy, wait!" my father cried. "I ain't losing nothing else to Wallace Porterfield!"

But I was already to my car. My father clung helplessly to one of the supporting posts of the porch as I drove away.

The anger continued to mount as I made my way toward Porterfield's house, a bloodred tide that swept me down the long, winding road to where I hoped to find the old sheriff sitting in malevolent splendor, still the evil king at the rotten heart of Kingdom County.

I'd already begun to imagine the terrible violence of the coming confrontation when I drew in upon the house and saw the flashing lights.

Lonnie's patrol car was parked in the driveway, along with two others from the State Police. An ambulance rested in the driveway, its double doors open.

I saw Lonnie standing beneath the great oak in his father's yard, three uniformed officers around him, and there, a few yards away, lying on his back on the green lawn, the enormous figure of Wallace Porterfield.

A uniformed officer strode toward me as I approached the house.

"We're not letting traffic through right now," he said when I came to a stop.

"What happened?"

"It's Wallace Porterfield," the officer said. "Somebody shot him."

I glanced toward the figure in the grass, the empty lawn chair beyond him, his now-vacant throne.

My father's voice gathered around me: *I ain't losing nothing else to Wallace Porterfield.*

He was standing uneasily in the backyard when I got back home, framed by the dense woods beyond him, a gaunt figure now with little left to waste away. He glanced toward me as I approached, then returned his gaze to the forest.

"I went to the store," I said when I stopped at his side. I took the package from my shirt pocket and held it out to him. "I thought you might be out of cigarettes."

He took the pack from my hand. "You go over to Porterfield's?"

"Yes, I did."

He opened the cigarettes, thumped one out. I lit it for him.

"Somebody shot him," I added.

He toed the ground with the tip of his boot.

I looked at him softly, watched as his eyes touched mine, then flitted away. "Saved me a world of trouble," I told my father.

We didn't speak of it again. Nor was the name of Wallace Porterfield mentioned in my father's house until Lonnie showed up at our door three days later.

"Roy, I need to ask you a couple of questions," he said.

I let him in, and for a moment he stared around, taking in my father's few battered possessions. I knew what he was thinking, that you could take a boy out of Waylord, but he'd always be the same, low and without ambition, doomed to make nothing of himself.

"Where's your daddy?"

"Sleeping." I nodded toward the couch by the window. "Have a seat."

He eyed the sofa as if it were a rotting stump. "No, I'll stand."

"What's on your mind, Lonnie?"

"I guess you must have heard about what happened to my daddy." His voice was a thin wire.

"Of course."

Lonnie's eyes fled toward the window. "Looks like somebody just drove up and motioned Daddy over," he said. "Best we can figure, when he got to the car, whoever it was just shot him in the head. With a thirty-eight. Shot my daddy point-blank."

I saw what I thought my father must have seen, Wallace Porterfield striding toward his car, leaning in, then the fiery blast, Porterfield stumbling backward, arms flailing, his face locked in dark wonder that Jesse Slater had come for him at last.

"So the thing is, Roy, I've been looking into it, you know? Checking various things, trying to figure out who might have done it. Daddy had lots of enemies, of course. A long list. But the thing is, well, I noticed something on his phone records. The thing is, he got a call real early last Wednesday morning. Now, Daddy's friends all know that he sleeps late. So I figured it couldn't have been a friend that called him. So I had the phone company run a check. And it turns out the call came from your daddy's phone. The one right here in this house."

I said nothing.

"Well, I got to thinking, and of course I know that there was bad blood between your daddy and my daddy. It goes back a ways, but bad blood is bad blood, if you know what I mean. And so, I have to ask about that call, Roy."

"I called your daddy," I said flatly.

"You called him?" Roy asked, surprised. "Why?"

"I wanted to ask him a few questions."

"About what?"

"About a whorehouse he ran over near Pittsville some years back. I was wondering how many girls he brought over there and raped."

Lonnie's face turned scarlet. "You have a gun, Roy?"

"Just an old rifle."

"I'm looking for a pistol."

"Then you're looking in the wrong place."

"I'll decide that," Lonnie said.

"Not without a warrant," I told him.

"I don't need a search warrant."

"Well, yes, Lonnie, actually, you do."

"Just where do you think you are, Roy?"

"I'm in my father's house," I said with a sudden shiver of pride. "And it's time for you to leave it."

"Do you think you can stop me from getting that gun?" His sneering laugh was exactly like his father's. "I can get a warrant and tear this place apart."

"Then go get your warrant."

Lonnie stared at me. "I'll be back," he said. "First thing tomorrow morning."

"I'll be waiting."

Lonnie glared at me but said nothing else, though I noticed that when he pulled out of the driveway, he turned on the siren to let me know just how powerful he was.

I waited until it died away before going into my father's room.

He started slightly when I shook him awake.

"Where's the gun, Dad?"

"Where it always is."

"I don't mean the rifle. The pistol. The thirty-eight."

He nodded toward the little table beside his bed. "Top drawer."

I opened the drawer and found it lying in a pile of matchboxes, old keys, whatever my father had thrown into the drawer over the last twenty years. The white evidence tag still dangled from its trigger guard.

"Lonnie's looking for this," I said.

"Then let him have it."

He'd said it with such indifference to the consequences that for an instant I wondered if he'd actually fired it three days before. I smelled the barrel and recognized the acrid scent: burnt powder.

"Give it to him, Roy," my father said. "It don't make no difference to me."

"He'll arrest you, Dad."

"So what? I'd get my three squares."

"I'm not letting him take you to jail."

"Why not?"

The truth came from me before I could stop it. "Because I want to be with you," I told him. "Until the end. And I'm going to make sure I can." I tucked the pistol into my belt just as my brother had done twenty years before.

I made my father's dinner a few hours later. He was too weak to make it to the kitchen, so I brought it to his bed. We talked awhile of nothing in particular, then he said, "What'd you do with that gun? Throw it into the creek or something?"

"No, they'd find it in the creek if they looked hard enough. Metal detectors could find it buried too. And I figure I'd be followed if I suddenly went for a drive."

"Where you gonna hide it, then?" my father asked.

"I have an idea," I answered. "I got it from a short story I read a long time ago."

"Helps you out, I guess," my father said. "All that reading."

He soon fell into a fitful sleep. By then it was night. I put on dark clothes, left the house, and for the next hour made my way through the woods surrounding Cantwell until I finally reached the long, wide lawn of Wallace Porterfield.

The garage wasn't locked, and so I entered it silently, found the box that contained the Kellogg file, and placed the pistol snugly among the other evidence of Archie's crime. Evidence concealed as evidence, like a letter hidden among other letters, with due thanks to Mr. Poe.

Then I stole back into the darkness, through the woods, and home.

Lonnie arrived the next morning with two deputies. I met him at the door.

"I've come for the gun," he said.

"And the warrant?" I asked.

He gave it to me, and I let him in.

"The gun's in my father's closet," I said. "He's sleeping in that room. Don't wake him."

Lonnie stomped into my father's room, rummaged through the closet, and found the rifle. Through it all I didn't hear my father stir.

"Is that rifle the only gun in the house?" he demanded when he returned to the front door.

"Yes, it is."

"You don't have a thirty-eight anywhere around? You swear that, Roy?"

I stiffened to attention, lifted my hand, mocking the stance he'd used when he deputized me two months before, and stared down at him coldly. "On my brother's grave."

Lonnie handed me the rifle. "One of these days I'll be coming back," he warned.

But he never did.

CHAPTER TWENTY-SIX

My father lived for three more weeks, and during that time I never left him again save for one brief trip to the library, where I checked out a book about how things work, how they are put together, everything from a spinning wheel to an electric generator. Each night I read to him from that book.

During that time, we stayed in his room together, not for minutes, but for hours, not only in the morning and the afternoon, but throughout the night, he in his bed, I seated beside it. His untroubled sleep comforted me, and my sleepless vigilance comforted him.

One night I awakened to find him staring at me silently, his face bathed in moonlight, an odd smile on his lips.

"What is it?" I asked.

One hand crawled into the other. "The balance," he said.

I buried him on a hot, sweltering day in the middle of August. Doc Poole came to the funeral, and a few of the men who'd once welcomed my father into their circle, lifting their bottles of beer to him and clapping him softly on the back as he moved among them. A few people came down from Waylord too, people I'd never known, nor even heard of. Lila came, but her mother didn't. "Mama died last week," she told me.

"I'm sorry to hear it," I said.

She nodded softly and offered her hand. "Well, goodbye, Roy."

I gave her no indication of what I'd learned from Mavis Wilde, but merely stood mutely at my father's grave and watched Lila walk out of the cemetery to where her old car baked in the hot summer sun. She got in and drove down the dusty road and away, falling, falling, as it seemed to me, into the web of Waylord.

It took nearly a month to sell the house, then another week to empty it in preparation for its new owners, a young couple with their first baby on the way.

During those long days, I gathered the few things my father had left behind, sold some of them to a local furniture dealer and burned the rest in a kind of funeral pyre behind the house.

After everything was settled, I packed my car with the single suitcase I'd brought with me nearly three months before, took the road that led once again past the old ball field, then through Kingdom City, and finally to the interstate highway whose westbound route led to California. Just before reaching it, a field of wildflowers rose to my right, weaving white and red in the summer sun. I pulled over and stared out over the field for a time. Then I set my mind on a different course.

She was in her garden when I found her, a soft mountain breeze playing at the hem of her plain white dress. She drew off the wide bonnet as I came toward her, hung it on a tomato post like a helmet over a rifle butt.

I handed her the flowers. "I picked them on the way up the road."

She brought them to her face. "You can smell the wildness in them. Not like the ones you buy in stores." She lowered her face toward the flowers again, then glanced up at me. "Thanks for coming by, Roy."

"My father thought I should have fought for you," I said.

She shook her head. "That was a long time ago."

"If you were willing, I'd stay around awhile. See how things work out."

She shook her head. "Roy, it's . . ."

"I know it's not exactly like jumping off a cliff behind you, but it's the best I can do. I'm not all that agile anymore."

She smiled.

"Lila — I know what you did for me."

Her smile faded, but in her eyes something wild and lovely bloomed.